Candy Story

European Women Writers Series

CANDY STORY

Marie Redonnet

TRANSLATED BY ALEXANDRA QUINN

University of Nebraska Press

Lincoln and London

Publication of this translation was
assisted by a grant from the French
Ministry of Culture.

Manufactured in the United States
of America. ♾ The paper in
this book meets the minimum re-
quirements of American
National Standard for Information
Sciences–Permanence
of Paper for Printed Library Mater-
ials, ANSI z39.48-1984.
Library of Congress Cataloging-in-
Publication Data
Redonnet, Marie [Candy story.
English] Candy story /
Marie Redonnet ; translated by
Alexandra Quinn.
p. cm. – (European women writers
series) ISBN 0-8032-3915-7
(alk. paper) I. Quinn, Alexandra,
1969-. II. Title. III. Series.
PQ2678.E285C3613 1996 843'.914–
dc20 95-10304CIP

Contents

Candy Story

To the memory of Judge Giovanni Falcone

Ma now lives at the Home in the Woods in Mells-le-Château. From her balcony all she can see are trees and the distant lake. Because she no longer sees clearly and confuses times and places, she thinks she has returned to Sise. Ma only remembers of Sise what she saw as a little girl from the window of Madame Alma's room; and what she saw was the sea, the sea so calm in Sise Bay that it seemed like a lake. Madame Alma, the mayor's widow, owned a house with a little tower. Ma called it the château. Now in her mind she confuses the Home and the château.

Today, June 21, is different from any other day because Ma and I were both born on the twenty-first of June. On her birthday Ma wanted to look her very best. She asked Mademoiselle Aldine, the nurse who takes care of her, to rinse and set her hair. Ma put on her prettiest suit, an exact copy of the original Chanel suit, to which she had added a little fur collar. Even though she has rheumatism in her arms and hands, she's still able to sew when she wants to alter a dress that she finds out-of-date. The suit is made of brushed silk and she wears it with an embroidered blouse, the same color as the headband Mademoiselle Aldine placed on her silver hair. Gold threads in the headband reflect nicely against her hair. Looking at herself in the mirror, Ma must have thought that on her birthday she resembled Madame Alma, a very elegant lady in her eyes though she was only the widow of the mayor of Sise. When Ma was little she spent her days with her best friend, Lou, the cook's daughter, pretending to be

an elegant lady.

Ma wears earrings for the first time, two fine pearls in the hollow of a little gold shell. She tells me the commander gave them to her this morning for her birthday. She is as thrilled as a young girl. The commander is the new resident at the Home and lives in the room next to her. When she goes out onto her balcony to water her flowers, they talk to each other. He tells her about his life as commander of the fort at Rore during the war. Ma listens with admiration. She sees him as a war hero – the person who saved the fort at Rore from the enemy. Ma would like to know everything about him. When it's dark and he thinks she's watching a nighttime soap opera on cable TV, she spies on him from behind the awning on her balcony. She turns up the volume so he won't think she's watching him. Just as the show begins and everyone at the Home sits down to watch, he goes out onto his balcony. He wears his thick, fur-lined coat and his long wool scarf so as not to catch cold, and he sits in his armchair with his back settled into the cushions. With large binoculars that date from his days as commander of the fort at Rore, he stares in the direction of the woods. Ma wonders what he could be looking at so intently. At that hour there are no horse races at the track and the bridle paths in the woods are deserted so it can't be the horses he stares at with his binoculars. Ma knows all about his passion for horses. It dates from his days as commander of the fort at Rore, where he was known as the best rider. When he could no longer ride he developed a passion for the races. He has never let Ma borrow his binoculars. He insists on his privacy. Their conversations always take place on the balcony. He has never invited her to his room, as if he didn't want her to see the inside. With Madame Aldine's theater binoculars, Ma has been able to see only as far as the traffic circle, where African women wearing leopard-skin shorts walk back and forth on the edge of the sidewalk and men slowly drive by, again and again. It cannot be the traffic circle that the commander watches with his binoculars. He could see all that every night on cable TV after midnight. Ma thinks he must have a secret. He must be watching something visible only to him beyond the traffic circle.

I wished Ma a happy birthday and gave her a present. I gave her a wristwatch that I bought on the Place Vendôme because Ma always told me that the best jeweler in Paris was on the Place Vendôme. She has never worn a watch before. She has always told time by her alarm clock that made the tick-tock she liked to hear. The alarm clock, which is very old, just broke and the watchmaker couldn't find the parts to fix it. Ma put the watch on her wrist. For her it's just a bracelet. She has no interest in the watch because it doesn't make a sound.

Ma wished me a happy birthday, also. She gave me a little box with a diamond inside, her only souvenir of Madame Alma, who never told her where the unset diamond came from. Ma had never told me about the diamond before. Then she gave me her second gift, the one she gives me every year – a check in an envelope. This time the check is bigger than usual, all the money in booklet A from her account at the savings bank. She wants me to take the unset diamond and the money from booklet A to the jeweler on the Place Vendôme to have a ring made, engraved on the inside: *Ma for Mia.* I have never worn a ring before.

Ma brought out a bottle of Laurent Perrier rosé from her little fridge and a cherry tart with vanilla cream that she bought at Fauchon. To her mind, there's no better treat in the world. She telephoned the commander to ask him over for a glass of champagne. This is the first time she has invited him to her room. She's so happy he accepted her invitation and so excited to introduce me to him. He's just as much of a gourmand as Ma. He doesn't speak much because he has tonsillitis and his voice is hoarse. He has on a cream-colored cashmere scarf and a black corduroy suit. He asked Ma whether she has started her watercolor painting. She said she would wait until after her birthday. Madame Alma taught her to paint and she has decided to take it up again. She asks him how his Memoirs are progressing. He has decided to begin all over again. Ma gazes at the commander with pride. She wants to take up watercolor painting again so that he will be proud of her as well. I told them I had to go and left the two of them together for the first time in Ma's room, to talk of their plans for the future.

§2

It's a direct trip from the station at Mells-le-Château to Paris-Notre-Dame, with one stop at Mills-le-Pont. Since the bank is still open I went to deposit my check. Curtz is at the window in front of me changing a wad of dollars into yen. He's wearing dark glasses and has a tan. I didn't know that he lived near Notre-Dame and that we were neighbors. He just returned from New York and is leaving for Tokyo to give a series of lectures on Witz. He's as rushed as ever. He didn't even have time to ask me how I was doing. He simply told me he hoped I would have a good vacation and said to call him at his office at Moréno when he returned. I realized then that it was not just my birthday but also the first day of summer. If Curtz had asked me where I was going on vacation, I wouldn't have known how to answer.

The one thing I know for sure is that I won't be reliving last summer's adventure when I took off to the Andes alone. I had suddenly decided to take the trip after having run into Curtz. Curtz wanted to meet me after having read *Sise Memories,* my first novel, which had just been published by Boston, Moréno's rival. He invited me for a drink at Seventies. I thought he wanted to talk to me about my novel, but no, the first thing he wanted to know was how much money I made. And right then and there he made me an offer to write an adventure novel about my summer vacation for his imprint at Moréno. Without even thinking, I decided to go to the Andes. Not only does Curtz have his own imprint at Moréno, he's also the most famous American novelist living in Paris who writes in French. I was very flattered that he was interested in me, even though he didn't mention *Sise Memories*. I wanted to please him by accepting his offer without further discussion and to seem interesting by leaving on my own for the Andes. It was the first time that anyone had invited me to Seventies since Boston had published my book. It was also the first time that I had received an advance substantial enough to take a leave without pay from the school where I taught in Mills-le-Pont. I saw Curtz as my benefactor. I thought only of him and the novel I would write for his imprint when I returned from the Andes. The minute I signed my contract with Moréno and received my advance, I bought my plane ticket to Lima.

Luckily I met Bobby Wick, another American, on the little train that climbed the Cordillera of the Andes. I had just felt faint from the sudden change in altitude when Bobby Wick, who was sitting next to me, immediately called the ticket collector, who made me breathe from the oxygen tank. Bobby Wick liked me as soon as I told him that I had published my first novel with Boston and that I had just signed a contract with Moréno to write my second novel, for Curtz's imprint. Bobby Wick and I spent the summer together. He was much older than I but knew how to make me forget that by telling me funny stories when I wanted to cry from always having to walk at such high altitudes in the bald mountains, where the clouds blocked any sight of a horizon. At night, in Bobby Wick's special high-altitude tent, which protected us from the glacial cold, we slept side by side in our down sleeping bags. I hadn't even thought to bring a tent, and without Bobby Wick I would have frozen to death one night all alone in the Andes. Bobby Wick told me that he had undergone a serious operation the previous year and was no longer able to have intimate relations. He had resigned himself to this loss after discovering the Andes, which for him were an ascension to the transcendence of his being. Over and over he repeated the word "transcendence" as if it were the word to end all words. Each night before going to sleep, he took notes in his black notebook for a poem that would live after his death. As a young man, he had come from America to study at the Sorbonne. That was when he sent his first manuscript to Boston. The novel was returned with a discouraging letter. That same year Curtz received a prize from Moréno for being the most talented young writer in France. Paris had no room for two American novelists who wrote in French: that was the way Bobby Wick justified his rejection, and he then decided to leave for Africa. Africa was his great passion, after the novel and before the Andes. In the Andes he was able to recapture his love for the novel through poetry, after his life in Africa had helped him to forget writing altogether. Now he believes that Paris may indeed have room for two Americans writing in French, Curtz for the novel and he for the poem. Bobby Wick considered our meeting in the Andes as a sign of fate. I understood, from what he said the night he told me about his operation and his inability to have intimate relations, that he had only been with Africans, never with whites. In Africa he contracted the terrible illness that nearly killed him. After his operation he left Africa for good. He couldn't live there without having intimate relations. Every night before I went to sleep, sensing that I was sad but not daring to ask why, he told me stories of Africa. It was as if he were under the spell of his memories. My deepest memories of my summer in the Andes with Bobby Wick are his memories of Africa. He told his stories as if they were pieces of a novel, and I asked him why he didn't write one for Curtz's imprint. He said his memories of Africa had nothing to do with a novel; they had to do with transcendence, with the poem he wanted to write before his death so that people would remember more than just Curtz's novels.

Each night Bobby Wick would massage my ankles, which were swollen because I had never walked in hiking boots before. Our last night on the Glacier of Angels was the most beautiful. For the first time the sky was completely free of clouds. All the stars were reflected in the blue glacier, and the sky was the glacier and the glacier was the sky. Then Bobby Wick spoke to me of God. For him God was the transcendental state that one attains after a long inward ascension, like being in the Andes and finally reaching the Glacier of Angels. At this moment, as he spoke to me of God, pressed against me as though he wanted to enfold me, I understood that, for the first time since his operation, he regretted not being able to have intimate relations. He would have wanted that night on the Glacier of Angels to be the final culmination of our meeting, a communion with the state he called God. When I returned to Paris I tried to write a novel about my summer in the Andes for Curtz's imprint at Moréno, but I couldn't. With my savings, I paid back the advance I had received, since I was unable to honor my contract. Curtz didn't answer my letter explaining that I had broken my contract because I couldn't write the novel he had hired me to write for his imprint.

It disturbed me to see Curtz again unexpectedly at the bank on my birthday, which is also the first day of summer. I haven't written anything all year, as if after *Sise Memories* I had nothing more to write. I couldn't bring myself to go back to teach grammar at the school in Mills-le-Pont. I went to see my doctor, Sonia, who put me on an extended sick leave. It's a real coincidence that as I left the bank I was thinking of my last summer in the Andes because right under my front door is a letter from Bobby Wick wishing me a happy birthday. He's too tired to go back to the Andes this summer but he hopes to come to Paris and see me again soon. The doorbell rang. I thought someone had sent me flowers for my birthday. It's just the mailman with a special-delivery letter from Sise.

Dilo and Lou were found drowned near the lighthouse in Sise. They were the same age as Ma. They've left me their house, which belonged to Ma's grandfather at one time and which Ma sold to them when she went to live at the Home. Ma gave me all the money from the sale, as if it were my inheritance. But I didn't know how to invest the money and have already spent most of it. Ever since Lou was little, her dream was to buy Ma's grandfather's house because she would have liked to be Ma, not Lou. She fulfilled her dream, and now I am inheriting Ma's grandfather's house for a second time. I have to leave for Sise immediately to be at Dilo and Lou's funeral tomorrow and to arrange things with my lawyer. I reserved a compartment in the sleeping car and packed my new summer dresses. My taste in clothes comes from Ma. She made dresses for herself just so she could dance in front of the mirror. When she taught me to dance she told me I had no talent for dancing.

§3

The overnight train leaves Paris at 11:05 P.M. as it always has but instead of arriving at Sise it now arrives at Sise City, the new city constructed after the swamp was drained. The Hotel by the Sea in Sise now belongs to Line, Marion's second daughter, while Lize built the Paradiso in Sise City. Last week there was a full-page article on the Paradiso in *Paris Night*, written by Witz. Witz is world famous for reinventing the spy novel and for making films of all his novels. He's also a great traveler, businessman, and gambler. He regularly publishes articles in *Paris Night* about his travels and the hotels where he stays while writing his novels, which he writes only during his trips. After discovering the Paradiso in Sise City, he decided to move there and devote himself to his Memoirs. Lize, having dreamed all her life of somehow becoming famous, must be very proud of that full-page article in *Paris Night*.

The overnight train is the same one I used to take to Sise with Ma every summer for vacation. To save money, Ma would buy third-class tickets without couchettes. We were so anxious to get to Sise that we could never sleep through the night. We drank hot coffee from a thermos and ate cherry tart with flaky crust and a layer of vanilla cream. We wiped our full mouths with flowery paper napkins, while lighted stations passed by in the night. When we arrived in Sise, Ma and I would get into Dilo's front-wheel-drive car. Lou would wait for us at Ma's grandfather's house. In anticipation of our arrival, she would have cleaned the whole house and stocked the pantry with provisions. She would also have prepared her special brioches filled with candied fruits. It was the first day of our vacation in Sise. Lou would be wearing her flounced dress with red and white polka dots in order to be admired by Ma, who always seemed to her to be elegance itself. Ever since Lou was little she had envied Ma, who was raised as the mayor's daughter by Madame Alma, while she, the cook's daughter, was already helping in the kitchen. Lou had no children because, she said, Dilo was sterile. Dilo adored Lou, who looked like a flamenco dancer, and he spent his life trying to please her in every way, never denying her anything. As a little boy, Dilo caught polio in the swamp and had felt diminished ever since. Lou was his revenge on life. He worked twice as hard driving his taxi so that she wouldn't have to work and could buy dresses from Paris and be the most elegant woman in Sise. In Dilo's mind, nothing was too good for Lou. He was so proud on Saturday nights when he would take her out for dinner at the Hotel by the Sea. When the music began, he would sit to the side and watch her dance. She would dance all night long with the commander of the camp, who preferred Lou to Marion.

For an instant, as the train left the station, I felt the same shiver of excitement as I had when I was a little girl sitting next to Ma. After leaving Paris, the train passes through Mills-le-Pont. In the distance I can see the red brick building where I lived on the very top floor with Ma for twenty-one years. As the train approaches the canal, it passes right by the place where Madame Irma's little house used to be. I would go to see her every Thursday; there were no classes that day and Ma was at work. Madame Irma was Madame Alma's sister. Ma had gone to live with her after Madame Alma died. Ma was angry at Madame Irma. She had never forgiven Madame Irma for making her the apprentice to a seamstress when she wanted to be a dancer. But Ma let me visit Madame Irma because of And, who lived there and gave me math lessons. Ma always wanted me to be first in my class so that I wouldn't ruin my life as she had by becoming a seamstress. After Mills-le-Pont, the train passes through Mells-le-Château, but the Home in the Woods is hidden behind the trees, and the train moves quickly out into the open countryside. I took *Aliza* from my bag – Curtz's latest novel, which I bought at the station before boarding the train. The inside jacket cover has a summary of the plot. The book sounds like a novel by Witz, as if Curtz were able to write only like Witz. It doesn't prevent Curtz from being very famous and successful.

I don't feel like reading *Aliza* or sleeping so I walked into the corridor. A passenger in a black leather jacket is standing in front of my compartment as if he were waiting to talk to me. Despite his dark glasses I recognized him right away as Rotz, who writes for *Paris Night* and is a reporter on cable TV. Ever since he went to America to do a story with Curtz, all he thinks of is writing his first novel. He feels that he has reached a turning point in both his life and his career. He's traveling to Sise City to do a story on Witz at the Paradiso. He wants to know who I am and what I'm going to do in Sise City. He has no idea I'm the author of *Sise Memories* because he only knows authors who have been interviewed by Erma on cable. I tell him that I'm going to Sise, not Sise City, for the funeral of Dilo and Lou, whose sole heir I am. Then, since I'm embarrassed all of a sudden to tell him that I arranged to be on an extended sick leave because I don't want to go back to teach at the school at Mills-le-Pont, I told him, without thinking, that I'm a brain surgeon. That seemed to impress him a lot. He looked at his watch. It's already time for him to go back to his compartment. He wants to start his first novel riding on the overnight train to Sise City.

The bar is empty. I ordered a mint tea. The bartender gave me his best smile and started to tell me about his childhood. I don't feel like listening to him because I already know what he wants. I gave him a tip and said good night. Despite the tip, he seemed very disappointed. He's a good-looking boy with black curly hair who is in the habit of having adventures on overnight trains. He can't understand why the adventure isn't going to happen tonight when he's so bored and alone at the bar. And after all, I can't tell him that after meeting Kell on an overnight train I promised myself never to have another affair on an overnight train. I have been trying to forget Kell ever since he left me without a word, but I cannot. I can't understand how, when our train arrived at the station, Kell could say goodbye as if he didn't know me, after calling me Candy all night as if he had known me forever. *Candy* was the song that Marion always sang at the Hotel by the Sea after having seen *The Paradiso of Fort Amo,* the film that Witz made of his first novel. It was also the name that Stev, the son of the lighthouse keeper, gave me one night on the beach at Sise during my eighteenth summer. Despite the bartender's disappointment, I left the bar. I quickly returned to my compartment and took two sleeping pills so that I would fall asleep right away and not think about Kell anymore.

§4

Sise City used to be the swamp the train passed over before entering the peninsula, at the very tip of which was Sise. The station was built at Sise only for the military base, which specialized in army maneuvers. The military base was surrounded by barbed wire fences with large signs – *Keep Out. Danger* – and drew no one to Sise. The Hotel by the Sea was frequented only by the officers-in-training who went to hear Marion sing. When the wind blew from the mainland, the noise from the rifle range, where the recruits trained from morning till night, made it sound as if there was a war in Sise. Neither Line nor Lize looked like Marion, and neither had a gift for singing. Line spent her days reading poems, which she read aloud to the officers at night. Lize's one desire was to leave Sise and the Hotel by the Sea to escape the noise from the rifle range, which gave her nightmares. She spent her days reading *Cinéview* and acting like Lill, the *Cinéview* model who became a star after appearing in Witz's first movie. Life for Lize was the movies covered in *Cinéview* and the love affairs of Lill and Witz. In her low-cut, brightly colored dresses Lize was very popular with the officers-in-training at the base, unlike Line, who bored them with her poems, none of which they understood.

The summer when she was twenty, Lize met Lenz, an officer-in-training who hated army maneuvers and spent his days in the infirmary reading *Cinéview*. When he first met Lize at the Hotel by the Sea he thought she was Lill, the model of his dreams. After dancing all night long, Lize and Lenz decided they were destined to be together. They dreamed of moving away from Sise and were searching for some project that would allow them to leave. In the meantime, they lived for their rendezvous at the boathouse near the lighthouse. Then Lenz heard about the project to drain the swamp. The commander of the base had secretly put in the request to headquarters because his men were dropping like flies during the army maneuvers. Almost all of them had sickness in their blood from fighting in the colonial wars. When Lenz heard that the project had been approved, he decided to take out a loan to buy all the unwanted swampland at a bargain price. He took a gamble that this speculation would make him a quick fortune. Lize and Lenz cared only about their project to create Sise City and become its leading citizens.

That same summer, Line met Will, Madame Alma's nephew. Line fell instantly head over heels in love. Will was a navy officer who came to live in Madame Alma's house in Sise after suffering from a serious illness he caught in the colonies. His two passions were the navy and the novel. After his illness, Will had to abandon the navy so he decided to devote himself to his second passion. He wanted to write the great novel on the colonial wars. Rumor had it that he invited young recruits to special evenings in the tower of Madame Alma's house. People said that the colonial wars had sent him over the edge and that he was doing the same to Line, who imitated him in everything.

That summer was unlike any other summer for me as well. After spending the day at the beach, Ma would finally leave me to visit Lou, and I would meet Stev. Ever since I began spending vacations in Sise, Stev and I would meet on the beach and stare into each other's eyes, without ever speaking because Ma wouldn't allow me to talk to the lighthouse keeper's son. That summer for the first time I disobeyed her – I secretly met Stev behind the boathouse every day after the beach. Stev would wait for me where the boards were uneven, leaving a crack through which you could see everything that went on inside. At that same hour, Lize and Lenz would have their rendezvous. We would look through the crack, watching everything they did inside the boathouse. As we watched, Stev would put my hand under his bathing suit for me to touch him and he would put his hand under my bathing suit, too, and touch me, harder and harder until Lize and Lenz started to scream and we would immediately pull our hands out. We would be flushed and dripping from the heat of the direct sun behind the boathouse, and would run away hastily, saying see you tomorrow. One day we forgot to be on the lookout and the lighthouse keeper caught us by surprise. He threatened to tell Ma everything if I ever saw Stev again, and he locked the boathouse.

Each night I went by boat with Dilo and Lou to the Island of the Birds, which helped me forget that I couldn't see Stev anymore. The commander of the base had a small house there, where he slept every night after the army maneuvers. Dilo would leave Lou at the door to the house, and he would take me for a walk around the island. He would recite the poems he wrote for Lou and I would blush uncontrollably, as though the poems were addressed to me. They were very short poems about Lou's breasts and hips. I could hide my embarrassment because it was nighttime, and Dilo never noticed. Then it would be time to pick up Lou and return to Sise. I was always sad when we got back because Dilo noticed only Lou, as if I no longer existed. Instead of leaving them, I would hide behind the tamarind tree and wait for the light in their bedroom window to turn on. I would watch Dilo take off Lou's dress, under which she wore nothing, and throw himself on her, kissing her breasts and hips. They would leave the window wide open because of the heat, and I could hear them moan louder and louder. When they began to scream I would cover my ears with my hands and run away.

One night, after having escaped from behind the tamarind tree where I was watching Dilo and Lou through the window, I ran into Stev leaving the Hotel by the Sea. He invited me to walk with him on the beach. It was my first walk at night on the beach in Sise without Ma. I couldn't see Stev in the darkness but I could feel him edging closer and closer to me. Every night since we were forbidden to meet behind the boathouse, he would go to the Hotel by the Sea to hear Marion sing *Candy*. He wrote his first poems for Marion, which Line then read to the officers, who for once applauded loudly. Now Stev wanted to live only for poetry and for Marion, for whom he wrote all of his poems. Suddenly he stopped talking and pushed me over on the sand. He unsnapped my sun dress. I opened my thighs which were all wet from his pressing so hard against me. He called me Candy as if he no longer knew who he was or who I was. After thinking about this alone every night as I watched Dilo and Lou from behind the tamarind tree, it was finally happening to me with Stev, whom I thought I would never see again. He made me moan, calling me Candy, until I forgot that I was bleeding and that my name was Mia. We parted quickly because I had to get home to Ma, who would be very worried that I was late. Stev said he would meet me on the beach the next day at the same time. When I arrived home, Ma was crying because she thought I had drowned by the lighthouse. I had a fever all night that lasted the entire summer. I never saw Stev again, and I never returned to Sise.

It's strange how all the memories of my last summer in Sise returned in my dreams last night on the train, as if the two sleeping pills were to blame. The train is passing over the heath of gorse and heather that once announced the approach of the swamp. The ticket collector banged on my door to say that we will arrive in Sise City in half an hour.

§5
Outside my compartment, in the corridor of the sleeping car, Rotz is filming the oil well in Sise City, with its flame

burning against the blue sky like a movie set. Sise City owes its rapid development to oil deposits discovered by a geologist who was in the navy reserves. Lenz, having just bought all the unwanted swampland, was extremely lucky. The exploitation of the deposits brought about the closing of the base. The officers retired early to go into the oil business. They founded Petroleum Associates Limited, known as PAL, and the former commander of the base became its president. PAL quickly diversified its business into import-export. During that time, Lize built the Paradiso, while Lenz, with profits from his land speculation, built the Palace by the Sea, which ran a casino day and night.

While Rotz is filming everything from the train window, I watch him without being seen. He's tall and thin and looks as if he belongs to a health club. He has changed his clothes since last night. He has on a raspberry-colored linen vest over an almond-green silk shirt with yellow stripes and tight-fitting white pants. He's purposely unshaven and with his dark glasses he looks exactly like the leading man in Witz's movies. He looked surprised when he saw me, as if he didn't recognize me. I changed too. I put on a bright yellow piqué dress with a black belt and gold sandals. I have a yellow headband in my hair, which is frizzy because I washed it without brushing it. Yellow is my favorite color for the beach because it goes well with blue and drinks in all the sunlight. I want to look pretty for my arrival in Sise City, even though I'm going to Dilo and Lou's funeral.

It was Ma who taught me to appear different from the way I feel. Even deeply unhappy with her life, which was ruined by Madame Irma, she always smiled and acted as elegantly as the flight attendant she would have chosen to be if she couldn't have been a dancer. In a certain way I resemble Ma. This morning, in my bright yellow piqué dress and my gold sandals, I'm cheerful and lighthearted to please Rotz. But in my heart I'm sad that Dilo and Lou are dead and that Ma is losing her mind. When she goes out alone, the police have to bring her back to the Home because she gets lost in the woods and can't find her way back. Ever since I was little, Ma has told me that the only thing of importance to her is for me to escape the curse of Sise. Some days I'm afraid the curse will overpower me and, rather than ruin my life like Madame Irma and Ma, I would prefer to drown myself in the Seine.

Rotz is in a good mood this morning because on the train last night he wrote the first thirty pages of his five-hundred-page novel on his portable Macintosh. He is focused on the pleasures of a week's break at the Paradiso in Sise City. Rotz enjoys life's pleasures. He indulges himself to forget his childhood in a poor section of Marseille. I enjoy life's pleasures as well, but unlike Rotz I can't afford them. If last night I had told him what I really do, instead of saying that I was a brain surgeon, he wouldn't be so friendly to me this morning. Nothing is more reassuring than a brain surgeon who removes the tumors that bring us madness and despair. Rotz shares with Witz and Curtz the philosophy that pleasure is everything, at any cost and by any means.

Leaving the train station I was overwhelmed by the light in Sise City, the same as in Sise. Rotz didn't want us to part just yet, so he invited me to have breakfast at the Paradiso. Dilo and Lou's funeral doesn't start until the afternoon, and I'm anxious to see Lize before I see Line, so I accepted his invitation. Also, I'm flattered to be arriving at the Paradiso with Rotz. Sise City has two centers: Town Hall and the import-export agencies, which face the station, and the point on which sit the Palace by the Sea and the Paradiso. Between the two is the amusement park, which like the casino is open day and night. Lenz, the mayor of Sise City since it was founded, is very proud of the design of his city. From the station to the Paradiso you take Park Avenue, which runs in a straight line to the Palace by the Sea, alongside the amusement park with its ferris wheel rising above Sise City. Neocolonial houses line Park Avenue. They are the homes of former officers from the Sise base who now work for import-export firms. From our taxi window, Rotz films everything. He's already working on his story. The Palace by the Sea, which is constantly being repaired, looks like an ancient theater with its marble columns and its facade overlooking the sea. Apparently its foundations were poorly built and, despite all the work to solidify them, they are still in danger of collapsing. Not even Lenz's profits from the casino can pay the ever-increasing bills for the continual repairs on the Palace by the Sea.

§6

Overlooking the Palace by the Sea, the bar of the Paradiso dominates the point. Lize doesn't have a minute to herself today. At noon, Lill and Witz are expected to arrive at the airport for the premiere of Witz's new movie, being held tonight at the Palace by the Sea. Rotz forgets about his breakfast. All his thoughts are focused on his exclusive interview with Witz tonight after the premiere. He doesn't want to be second-best all his life. While Rotz waits his turn for success, he learns from Witz and Curtz. When Witz is away from Paris, he never leaves the Paradiso. The hotel reserves most of its rooms for Witz's friends from the movies and business, whom he needs to keep by his side. Witz made his fortune not only by writing novels and making movies but also by investing wisely. Unfortunately, living in Sise City, all the money he makes he loses at the casino. Before coming to Sise City, Rotz looked into PAL, which is close to bankruptcy and on the point of being repurchased by the Bank of Rore. The bank's president is also the mayor of Rore and the man who lent Lenz the money to pay for the continual repairs on the Palace by the Sea. The Bank of Rore is buying all the land for sale in Sise City.

I recognized Lize right away. She looks even more like Lill than before. Lize is very proud to have Lill at the Palace by the Sea for Witz's premiere. When Lize and Lill stand side-by-side on the podium, no one will be able to tell them apart. Rotz didn't hide his surprise at their resemblance. Lize was very flattered because her great source of pride is looking so much like Lill that people confuse them. The Paradiso in Sise City brings to life *The Paradiso of Fort Amo,* Witz's film in which Lill played Candy, the unforgettable role that made her a star. By building the Paradiso in Sise City, Lize could imagine herself as Lill living on the set of *The Paradiso of Fort Amo.* Lize speaks to Rotz as if she were playing the role of Lill before a hidden camera. There has been an attraction between them since the moment they met. I'm in the way. I thought Rotz was interested in me last night when I told him I was a brain surgeon, but that's over. He's interested in Lize now, not me. Lize hasn't been the same since Witz moved to the Paradiso with all his friends. She's familiar only with authors recommended by Erma on cable TV, and she doesn't know that I published *Sise Memories* with Boston. When Rotz told her that I was a brain surgeon, she said that had always been my vocation.

I asked Lize whether she was coming with me to Dilo and Lou's funeral. She said no. She doesn't want to dwell on the death of Dilo and Lou on the same day that Lill is arriving for Witz's premiere. Lize did invite me to tonight's reception at the Palace by the Sea. She is full of pride because Witz told her that she figures in his Memoirs. To her mind, Witz's Memoirs will be the great event of the end of the twentieth century. In his Memoirs, Witz tells of his experience as an aviator in the war. This is the first time I've ever been invited to a reception with Witz. But I'm going as a brain surgeon, not as the author of *Sise Memories,* which makes everything different. It's as if life in Sise City is a movie and I have only to play my part. I think of Witz as the creator of *The Paradiso of Fort Amo.*

Rotz takes advantage of the moment when Lize is called to the phone to tell me that Lill is having an affair with Curtz. In Paris, the hatred between Witz and Curtz is the talk of the town. Witz is the one who for now keeps Curtz from being considered the best. Winning Lill's heart is certainly part of Curtz's plan. Without Lill, Witz would no longer be Witz. Rotz also tells me that Witz can no longer live without Lize, who has made herself indispensable by organizing special evenings at the Paradiso. Rotz thinks that Lize has a dual personality and he wants to know if I agree. I reply that I don't know what it means to have a dual personality. He seems bored, as if he thinks I lack any personality. He keeps looking toward the phone, as if he were trying to guess who Lize could be talking to for so long.

Rotz offered to accompany Lize to the Palace by the Sea to make the final preparations for the premiere. Lize insisted on lending me a car to drive to Sise. I stayed at the bar alone. I could almost pretend that I was at the Paradiso in Fort Amo and Lill was singing *Candy*. It's time for me to leave for Sise for Dilo and Lou's funeral. I mustn't forget that I came to Sise for them and to take care of their affairs, because for the second time I have inherited Ma's grandfather's house.

§7

I chose an automatic Golf GTI to take me from the Paradiso to Sise. The road rises up on the peninsula. The tide is going out. Mussels and seaweed cover the rocks where the sea has receded. Oleanders in full bloom line the side of the road. The warm current creates a microclimate in Sise. The meeting of the warm current and the swamp once made Sise the most unhealthy region on the coast. Now that the swamp has been drained, the current is the pride of Sise. The Golf GTI is a convertible. I put the top down just like in one of Witz's movies, where there's always a scene of a convertible Lancia driving on a mountain road. I can't believe that I'm driving to Dilo and Lou's funeral. The road to Sise was rebuilt to serve the airport. In my bright yellow piqué dress and my dark glasses, I look like a tourist in the country on her way to pick up her fiancé at the airport. But I'm not a tourist, and I have no fiancé.

The road is not the same as I remember it from the days when Dilo would drive me in his front-wheel-drive car.

He hoped that a front-wheel drive would make him seem like a race car driver so that Lou, sitting at his side, would be proud of him. In those days the road was narrow and dangerous on the edge of the cliff without a guardrail. The officers from the base used to race each other in jeeps, and there were frequent accidents. The road had a bad reputation. Dilo drove fast to prove to himself that he could have raced cars if he hadn't had to drive a taxi. I never told him that his driving made me feel sick, because I liked being in Lou's seat alone in the car with Dilo. The road used to run past the military base, which had barbed wire fences and signs everywhere with red letters surmounted by a black skull that warned: *Keep Out. Danger.* Now the airport runway has replaced the rifle range of the old military base. I read in *Paris Night* that Witz has just purchased a jet that he flies himself. At noon, he and Lill are going to land at the airport in his brand-new jet. I would never have known about the affair between Lill and Curtz had I not run into Rotz.

As the road descended toward Sise, my heart began to beat as it did when I was a little girl. Looking down from the cliff, I could see the same blue-shuttered houses covered with Virginia creeper facing the islands, and beyond them the sea made rough by the reefs. If it weren't for the channel between the two islands, Sise Bay would be enclosed and the sea a lagoon. At low tide, the islands link together like a great ring that closes the bay, broken only by the channel. Everyone in Sise owns a boat to go to the islands. The smaller one, the Island of the Birds, is covered in woods that shelter many unusual species. It was on this island that the commander built the little house where he would meet Lou. The larger island, the Island of the Dead, is entirely rocky and takes its name from the cemetery that the people of Sise located there to avoid the swamp, which lay so close to town. It's one of the peculiarities of Sise that the town's church is also on the island; the people wanted it near their cemetery. Father Jan was the only person who lived on the Island of the Dead. Every Sunday, the whole town went to mass by boat. Father Jan commented not on the Bible but on his dreams that God had inspired him to guide the people of Sise. He explained his dreams as though they were modern parables that God had chosen the people of Sise to hear. Every Sunday during mass, Marion sang the hymns all alone in Sise's ancient language, which no one understood anymore. To hear Marion's voice without understanding the words added to the magic. It was during my last summer in Sise that Marion decided to leave the Hotel by the Sea to live near Father Jan on the Island of the Dead.

Ma used to tell me that the people of Sise were different because their ancestors came from far away. After a great shipwreck, they passed through the channel in a lifeboat to reach the uninhabited bay of Sise. Ma would tell me how the ship's captain, who escaped in his boat, was the first man to discover America. However, his discovery went with him to the grave and his name remained unknown. The captain's son, who commanded the lifeboat, was Ma's grandfather's ancestor and became the keeper of the lighthouse in Sise, which was named after him. In order to preserve the family name, Ma never married, and I used the same name to sign *Sise Memories*. Ma was very proud to be a descendant of her grandfather from Sise. She told me never to forget that her grandfather's ancestor discovered America and that his son founded Sise. She told me this story so that I would forget that her grandfather was found drowned near the lighthouse with Madame Alma. She also wanted me to forget Madame Irma, who ended her life at the rest home in Mills-le-Pont, after having ruined Ma's life by making her an apprentice to a seamstress when she had wanted to be a dancer.

I was born and raised in Mills-le-Pont but I feel as though I come from Sise because Ma always told me this legend as if it belonged to me as well as to the people of Sise. Without such a legend, how could they have survived the swamp that brought them illness, the military base that brought them troubles, and the reefs that brought death to their best seamen? There were always affairs between the girls from Sise and the officers from the base, who thought they were allowed to do anything they wanted. The base was the center for smuggling all sorts of things through the channel. The police closed their eyes because the commander was protected by top officials. The base made Sise an undesirable place to live. Even though we were on vacation, Ma would watch over me all the time like she did in Mills-le-Pont. She was afraid that I would make a mistake and ruin my life like the girls from Sise who, after having been taken dancing at the Hotel by the Sea, would leave for Paris to become dancers, only to end up in the Salpêtrière. Ma said the colonial wars were to blame for the hidden wounds and the shame of the Sise base.

Of all the nights in the summer, Ma went out only for the ball on July 14. It was held in the town square, which was illuminated with all of its street lamps. That night, the commander of the base opened the ball not with Lou but with Ma. They made a good couple. Ma was the most elegant one in her white muslin dress, wearing gold pumps and a red rose in her hair. Her eyes sparkled while she danced with the commander, as if the dance would never end, and she was now and forever the dancer of her dreams. Throughout the dance, I would sit next to Dilo and watch her dance. Ma would leave the ball after the fireworks because she didn't want me to go to bed late. She must remember the commander from Sise, with whom she so enjoyed dancing the night of July 14, while now, at the Home, she talks to the former commander of the fort in Rore.

I parked the Golf GTI in front of the Hotel by the Sea. Madame Alma's old house, where Ma lived happily with Lou for twelve years, is next to the hotel. Like the front of the house, the facade of the hotel is covered in Virginia creeper. It would be impossible to distinguish one from the other if the house didn't have its little tower and the hotel its sign. Both buildings have a back view overlooking the islands, and they share a single garden, separated only by a rose hedge. The sea is the color of a lagoon. There are no waves, nothing but gentle ripples. The officers from the base used to appreciate the Hotel by the Sea with its rooms facing the islands. They would spend their nights on leave at the hotel with girls from Sise, whom they called their fiancées. The officers-in-training rented the rooms facing the square, which had only washbasins. Marion always knew to whom she should rent each room, and all her rooms were always rented several weeks in advance. She refused to rent any rooms at all to the recruits because she wanted to maintain a good clientele.

§8

Line waits for me in the garden. She's wearing a loose-fitting white crêpe dress, the same as always. She immediately mentioned *Sise Memories,* which Lou had given to her to read aloud. Lou lost her sight toward the end of her life, and Line would read to her. Line made it clear to me that she hasn't had a happy life. She wasn't born to run a hotel. The only people to frequent the Hotel by the Sea anymore are pilots from the airport, who stay there when they have a stopover in Sise. Nothing happens in the hotel; people are only passing through. Now the Paradiso in Sise City gets all the business. Will died a year ago, leaving Madame Alma's house to Sise City. He gave up writing his great novel on the colonial wars because, instead of taking away his pain, writing only made it worse. As his pain grew worse he made Line suffer more, which only increased his pain. He accused himself of crimes he hadn't committed because, in the end, he convinced himself that he had. The young recruit who was completely devoted to him died of the same pain several months later. Line was never happy with Will. Stev is her only friend. He never left Sise because Marion was there, the person for whom he wrote all his poems. Moréno and Boston both refused to publish his poems. They asked him to stop writing poetry and to write a novel about Marion's life. But for Stev poetry is all that counts. He never married. He is now the lighthouse keeper and lives closed up in the lighthouse, writing poems to Marion. Line is the only one who reads them. She copies all the poems secretly for fear that one day he might throw them in the sea. Line says that Stev's poems make up the story of his life.

Dilo and Lou received many offers for their house, some even large enough to ensure their security for life, but they refused to sell. Dilo wanted me to have something of theirs after their death. Lou wanted to allow me to reclaim my heritage. She didn't believe that I knew how to invest my money, and she thought that I must have already spent most of the money from the sale of Ma's grandfather's house. Lou never forgot the humiliation she felt as a little girl at being the cook's daughter. Her last revenge was to leave Ma's grandfather's house to me, which she had bought only so I would inherit it a second time. Lou was an important person in Sise City because she was having an affair with the president of PAL. Dilo became the president's chauffeur and PAL's confidential secretary. In exchange for the services that PAL could ask only of Dilo – since he was the only one who could perform them – they gave him large sums of money, which he invested in the stock market. The president couldn't live without Lou. He showered her with jewelry and furs and brought her on all his trips. It was only a year ago that Dilo and Lou retired to Sise to live in Ma's grandfather's house.

Line arranged Dilo and Lou's funeral according to their last wishes. In the end, Lou and Line were inseparable despite their age difference. Line read aloud to Lou all the classics that Lou had never read. Lou left Line the journal that she had kept throughout her life without Dilo's knowledge, and she asked Line to rewrite it as a classic to be published after her death. Line says that unfortunately Lou's journal cannot be rewritten, that none of it is worth publishing. While Line read the classics to Lou, Dilo read business magazines in an attempt to understand why he lost all the money he invested in the stock market. While reading he would fall asleep suddenly. He was able to live only with the aid of the tranquilizers and analgesics he took for the intense pain caused by the paralysis spreading in his legs.

Dilo and Lou are the last people of Sise to be buried on the Island of the Dead because there is no more room in the cemetery. From now on, the people of Sise will be buried in the new cemetery, which runs along the railroad tracks. One of Dilo and Lou's last wishes was that only Line and I be at their burial. Their coffins are already at the cemetery, ready to be lowered into the grave dug this morning at dawn. For the funeral I put on a blue suit and a white hat to match my flats. I ran to meet Line at the dock because she had told me that funerals in Sise City are very organized and punctual, and not to be late.

It's only now, in the boat on our way to the Island of the Dead, that Line tells me how Dilo and Lou died. To her mind, it's the most beautiful death, the final chapter of the novel that Lou never wrote because her life was her novel. Dilo and Lou decided to die together when they discovered that they would have to move to the nursing home in Sise City. Lou was blind and Dilo's paralysis was spreading throughout his body. Dilo, who spent his life compensating for having had polio as a child, didn't want to end up confined to bed, even a luxurious one in the nursing home, with Lou blind at his bedside. They decided to take their boat out one stormy night through the channel to the open sea, and capsize where the current flows back to the lighthouse. The current always brings drowned bodies to Sise. Dilo's and Lou's bodies were found the next day just as they had predicted. They were attached by a rope so they wouldn't be separated from each other. Line believes that Dilo and Lou felt the deepest love possible because they were inseparable through death, and beyond.

I asked Line how she could know about Dilo's and Lou's deaths as if she had been there herself. A few days before they died, Line read to Lou the final pages of a manuscript she had found at the bottom of the large trunk in Dilo and Lou's house. Ma never wanted to open the trunk, using the excuse that the keys were lost and the lock would have to be forced open. It was Dilo who opened it without forcing the lock at all. The trunk contains all the books that the bookseller in Sise was unable to sell, which Ma's grandfather bought for practically nothing. The books are the memoirs of the sailors from Sise. Those who lived through the frequent storms in the sea full of reefs wrote down stories of their voyages, which the bookseller published at the sailors' expense. Most of the books are torn. Sometimes only a few pages remain, like those that Line read to Lou. Lou told Line that she had just finished reading the story of Dilo's and her death, as though it had already been written.

Dilo and Lou's burial was short. They requested in their will to be buried without religious ceremony because Father Jan was dead and his teachings were their only religion. They underlined in red pen that they wanted no religious ceremony and no wreaths because wreaths are too funereal. Dilo and Lou's decision to drown, by capsizing their boat where the current would be sure to wash them to Sise, marks the beginning of their second life on the Island of the Dead, where the birds singing on the neighboring island sound like a concert in the heavens. The funeral followed the will precisely. An engraver from Sise City carved on their tombstone: *Here lie Dilo and Lou, who loved each other in life as they love each other in death.* It's the last sentence in Lou's journal, the only one that will ever be published. Of all the poems that Dilo wrote for Lou, the last one will remain, carved on the tombstone as an epitaph: *For Lou, my soul, in the eternity of death.* Dilo and Lou are buried at the edge of the island, next to the sheer cliff. They look out over the open sea, not the land.

I told Line that I wanted to stay there alone. At low tide I will walk back. The only person still living on the island is

Marion, who is completely blind. Marion has lived alone with the dead since Father Jan died. Stev visits her every day. He reads her his latest poems, which he writes for her as he has since she used to sing *Candy* at the Hotel by the Sea. The Island of the Dead with its many flowers doesn't seem like a cemetery. When Father Jan was alive, he wrote the epitaphs for all the tombstones. He wanted Sise to be remembered for its cemetery, which is like a poem carved on tombstones. The little church is closed, but the key to the front door is hidden under a stone so that people can still visit it. Inside is the old fresco, which is not entirely discolored, depicting the sails of the great sinking ship, its bow all that is visible, and amidst the waves the lifeboat full of survivors.

It did me good to collect myself all alone by Dilo and Lou's grave. I didn't try to remember anything, only to collect myself. Marion must have thought that no one was left in the cemetery because she approached slowly. She stopped right next to me in front of Dilo and Lou's grave. Then she began to sing the song that Ma used to sing to me during our vacations in Sise to fight off night-mares and welcome sweet dreams. It's a song without words. I closed my eyes and listened to Marion as though I were falling asleep in Ma's arms once more. The tide began to recede. Without making any noise that would disturb Marion, I said goodbye to Dilo and Lou and left the Island of the Dead.

§9

Before returning to the Hotel by the Sea to say goodbye to Line, I went to Dilo and Lou's house at the edge of Sise. I will always think of the house as belonging to Ma's grandfather. Ma was very close to her grandfather. She would go to see him every day in his lighthouse. He would teach her how the equipment worked, and she would polish it to shine like new, even though the lighthouse was old and the equipment worn. With her grandfather's large binoculars, Ma would watch the boats pass by Sise as they followed the maritime route to Rore. Ma talked about her grandfather having been found drowned with Madame Alma near the lighthouse. I can't bring myself to think of Ma's grandfather's house as my own. I have never owned a house.

The facade of the blue-shuttered house, covered in Virginia creeper, hasn't changed. The key is in the mailbox where we always left it when we would go out. Ma never worried about burglars because she said there was nothing in her grandfather's house worth stealing. The inside hasn't changed either; everything is the same, right down to the collection of tiny porcelain animals arranged neatly on the large sideboard. In the bedroom, above the bed hangs the framed photo of Ma's grandfather in his lighthouse keeper's uniform. It was taken the day he received a medal of merit for rescuing a young recruit, who had wanted to end his life in the sea. Next to it is a smaller

photo of Madame Alma holding Ma on her knees. Because the photographer was an amateur, the picture is out
of focus and Ma blends into Madame Alma's dress. Lou's dresses fill the armoire in the master bedroom. They are evening dresses, each with its own fur stole, pair of sandals, gloves, and bag to match. With the money Dilo made from PAL, he was able to buy for Lou the dresses she dreamed of as a girl looking through Madame Alma's fashion magazines. Dilo and Lou's special relationship with the president of PAL brought them invitations to all the receptions, as though they themselves were important. When I think of who they were when I knew them in Sise, I can't believe who they became in Sise City. Had Lou remained in Sise with Dilo for her entire life, nothing would have changed, and Dilo would have continued to drive a taxi though he longed to race cars. The establishment of Sise City presented them with the chance of a lifetime, which they seized without hesitation. As chauffeur to the president of PAL, Dilo lived in the little house next to the garage at the edge of the president's property with its grand villa on the hill. Lou divided her time between the little house and the grand villa. With the money that Dilo made performing important duties for PAL, he and Lou could have bought their own pretty villa on the hill. But Dilo preferred to invest his money in the stock market. Dilo and Lou wanted to spend their final days in Ma's grandfather's house in Sise, not in a pretty villa on the hill in Sise City.

I remained for a long time sitting in the rocking chair in front of the window facing the Island of the Birds. Ma would sit in this chair every night and read aloud the classics, which were neatly arranged on her grandfather's desk. He had read all the classics, hoping to leave the Sise lighthouse to become a teacher. Each year Ma would reread the classics to me because they are timeless, and in order to succeed in school I had to know them by heart. But I wasn't listening to her as she read. I was dreaming of Stev and of all that we had said to each other on the beach just by looking into each other's eyes. Thinking back to my nighttime outings to the Island of the Birds with Dilo and Lou, I can't understand how Dilo, who was so in love with Lou, could leave her at the commander's little house and take me on a tour of the island, reciting his poems to me as if I were the one for whom they were written. When Dilo met Lou again in front of the house, it was as if nothing had happened. He recited his poems to her and I no longer existed. Later, as I watched secretly from behind the tamarind tree while they made love by the wide-open window, why did they turn on all the lights and attract mosquitoes, as if they needed me to be there watching them, just as the cameraman and technicians watch a love scene during the making of a movie? Also, I can't understand why Ma, who never let me out of her sight all day long for fear I might do something that would ruin my life, let me go with Dilo and Lou every night to the Island of the Birds without ever coming along. She must have known that Lou went to meet the commander and that I would be alone with Dilo, because she and Lou told each other everything. With her large binoculars, she must also have been able to see everything that took place inside their little house with all the lights on. Maybe she simply needed to be alone for a moment in the darkness, to rest a bit and contemplate life.

I closed up the house and replaced the keys in the mailbox. If I sell the house, I will sell it with all the furniture just as it is. What would I do in Paris with all of Lou's evening gowns? The only thing I took with me was a photo taken at the ball on July 14. It's the best picture I've ever seen of Ma. She's the only one in the picture, and she's smiling a smile I don't recognize. This is the smile that I want to remember. I didn't go as far as the lighthouse. Line told me that she was sad I was leaving already because she feels alone in Sise now that Dilo and Lou are dead. She's considering closing the Hotel by the Sea. She wants to change her life but is not sure what to do. I will never return to Sise. For me now, Sise is only *Sise Memories.*

§10

The Paradiso is deserted because everyone is at the Palace by the Sea. I arrive too late to attend the screening and too early for the reception. So I have all the time I need to take a bath. The walls of the room are covered with photos of Lill in her various roles. The resemblance between Lize and Lill is increasingly striking with each one. When Witz discovered the Paradiso in Sise City, he must have thought he was dreaming. I want to look good this evening to be introduced to Witz. I can't allow myself to drink too much champagne and forget that I'm a brain surgeon. Tonight for the first time, I'm going to wear the Givenchy dress that I bought on sale last year. It's a full-length, sea-green tulle dress with slits at the sides, pearls encrusted along the edges, and a very low-cut neckline.

I received two shocks when I turned on the television to watch the news. There had been a tragedy at the Palace by the Sea. During his rounds, a fireman in charge of security discovered Lill's body horribly mutilated in one of the bathrooms. Witz, having just lost the remainder of his fortune at the casino, had disappeared. Both the screening of the film and the reception have been canceled. I put my Givenchy dress back in my suitcase. Lenz gave a brief statement announcing that the investigation will be conducted by Interpol, not the police department of Sise City. Lenz also stated that while Witz was living at the Paradiso in Sise City, he was also being treated at the psychiatric clinic for manic-depression. The president of PAL was recently admitted to the nursing home after suffering a stroke and Lind, his loyal private secretary, has disappeared. All of a sudden I saw Kell on the screen getting off the Interpol plane. How could I have known that he worked for Interpol since he never told me who he was?

I remember it was snowing, the plains were white through the fog, and snowflakes collided against the train windows. I was returning from a colloquium on disengagement in novels published by Boston, at which I hadn't said a word because as soon as I'm invited to a colloquium I can't think of what to say. A passenger was standing next to me in the corridor. He offered me a chocolate, having just quit smoking. I couldn't see his face very well because it was half hidden by the collar of his overcoat, which he had pulled up as though he were cold. He wasn't talkative. He didn't say what he did for a living. I didn't ask him any questions. We were alone in the corridor of the sleeping car. For a long time we stood side by side watching the snow fall. Then, bluntly he asked me into his compartment. He turned off the lights, even the night-light, and asked me to undress. I obeyed without saying anything, until he pushed me down on the carpet, calling me Candy. I don't know what I felt, having been Mia for so long, forgetting that I was Candy for Stev one night on the beach in Sise. The train passed through stations without stopping. At each station the compartment lit up and I could see the passenger who looked at me in a way I wished I understood. I couldn't have known then that I would find him again six months later in Sise City on the day of Dilo and Lou's funeral, after Lill had been found dead in the bathroom of the Palace by the Sea.

Lize walked into my room without knocking, followed by Rotz. Witz disappeared with the manuscript of his Memoirs. Lize is in a state of shock, as though it were her body that was just found in the bathroom of the Palace by the Sea. Rotz has already forgotten about his story on Witz at the Paradiso. The novel he started on the overnight train to Sise City is suddenly taking shape because he has just found his subject and his main character. He wants to reinvent the police novel just as Witz reinvented the spy novel. He is even more interested in Lize since the tragedy at the Palace by the Sea, and he follows her everywhere, unable to leave her side.

I put on my black dress with the lizard-skin belt and pearly buttons that I was wearing the night I met Kell on the train. Having just arrived in Sise City, Kell will certainly go to the bar at the Paradiso for a drink. I'm not mistaken. It's as if he were waiting to meet me at the Paradiso in Sise City. I asked him why he didn't want to see me after our affair on the overnight train. He told me that he was letting fate take its course because he believes in destiny. He can't see me in Sise City because of the investigation but will call me as soon as he returns to Paris.

I called my lawyer to tell him that I'm putting Dilo and Lou's house on the market. I want to arrange everything by correspondence without having to return to Sise. My lawyer said that it isn't a good time to sell. I said it doesn't matter because I want to sell anyway. Before calling a taxi to take me to the station to catch the train back to Paris, I turned on the television to see the latest news. Witz's jet crashed off the coast of Sise City right after takeoff. Witz and his Memoirs disappeared at sea. Witz's accident and Lill's death are still mysteries. The anchorman is visibly emotional. In his opinion no one will replace either Lill, the greatest actress and the one who immortalized the role of Candy, or Witz, the author of *The Paradiso of Fort Amo*.

I'm very emotional as well. I returned to Sise not just to attend Dilo and Lou's funeral and to take care of their affairs, as I thought. I also returned to find Kell, whom I thought I had lost, at the very moment that, as the anchorman said, the world was faced with the deaths of Lill and Witz, and the end of an era.

§11

I rented this minuscule studio with the sloping ceiling for its view of Notre-Dame, because Notre-Dame is where Ma and I used to go on our Sunday walks through Paris. I watch the news every day on cable. Sise City was the top story for a week but now it's as if the town no longer existed. Lill's terrible death in the bathroom of the Palace by the Sea and the disappearance of Witz's jet off the coast of Sise City have attracted a lot of publicity for Boston, the publishers of Witz's novels. In just a few days all Witz's books sold out and had to be reprinted. His novels are becoming the best-sellers of the summer – gaining popularity over Curtz's book *Aliza*. Retrospectives of Witz's films starring Lill are playing in theaters everywhere. Though Boston may have its best sales ever this summer, Witz's death means the loss of their most famous author. Witz's Memoirs disappeared at sea, so Boston won't be able to publish a posthumous edition, which might have allowed them to crush Moréno. Moréno will surely take advantage of this opportunity to make a comeback.

I decided to visit Ma. I didn't tell her that I went to Dilo and Lou's funeral or that I inherited her grandfather's house for the second time, because she thinks that Dilo and Lou have been dead for a long time and that her grandfather's house belongs to Madame Alma. I telephoned to tell her I was coming like I do whenever I visit, to give her time to make herself look nice for my arrival. Her phone is busy. So I called Mademoiselle Aldine to ask her to tell Ma I'm coming. As I arrived along Woods Lane, which runs past the racetrack, Ma wasn't on her balcony to greet me. Her shutters are closed. If she were sick, Mademoiselle Aldine would have told me.

I knocked, and as I entered the room Ma didn't even turn her head to see who it was. She's seated in front of her television. The set is on but the screen is black. Ma must have tuned into a nonexistent channel. I have never seen

Ma like this. Her room is dark. She hasn't brushed her hair, and she's still in her nightgown although it's early afternoon. I opened the shutters to let light into the room. All of a sudden I saw Ma as I have never seen her before. Through her nightgown, which is practically transparent and not properly buttoned, I can see her thin, white body with all its blue veins. Her breasts have disappeared and her skin is withered. I wanted to close my eyes and not see what has become of Ma. It's as if she wants to show me that her appearance no longer means anything to her. With no makeup and mussed hair, her face looks wrinkled and so pale. Softly, so as not to wake her, I kiss her and ask how she is as if she were having a bad dream. She lets me kiss her but seems not to hear me.

Her easel stands in one corner of the room with a painting propped against it. Ma started watercolor painting again as she said she would. The painting is quite clumsy but the effect is striking. It's Ma's self-portrait. One half of the face is the one she reveals now, which she must have painted by looking at herself in the mirror. The other half is Ma as a young girl, as she looked in a photo taken with Madame Alma. The photo is in the album on her coffee table, the one she would point out each time I came to visit. The painting is signed "Ma" in large letters painted in black so they can be clearly seen. The signature could be that of a little girl who just painted her first picture but still doesn't know how to write her name.

I went to ask Mademoiselle Aldine what had happened to Ma to put her in this state. Mademoiselle Aldine is the only one at the Home to whom Ma confides her secrets. Several days after Ma's birthday, the commander was rushed to the hospital after spitting up blood. He died of widespread cancer without ever regaining consciousness. Mademoiselle Aldine wanted to hide it from Ma. But as soon as Ma saw that the commander's balcony remained vacant, she said she knew everything and there was no point in making up stories. She'd suspected for months that the commander had throat cancer. Right up to the end she pretended that she didn't notice anything because he didn't want her to know, and she didn't want to ruin their time together by admitting that she knew. Now that the commander is dead, Ma spends her days sitting in front of her television watching the black screen. Now that he is dead she also calls Mademoiselle Aldine "Mia." Ma told Mademoiselle Aldine that Mia was Madame Alma's nickname, something she never told me. Ma now thinks that Mademoiselle Aldine is Madame Alma. Mademoiselle Aldine is touched because it's the first time in her life that she has ever had a nickname. She and her sister were raised in an orphanage and she has remained single, devoting her life to the Home. She has almost reached retirement age and she looks like an old doll. Every evening Madame Aldine brings Ma her herbal tea and sits by her side until Ma falls asleep.

The commander was buried at the military cemetery in Rore, according to his will. Because he has no heir, his belongings were turned over to the Home, which donated them to the needy. He had no valuable possessions aside from his binoculars. He never told anyone they were broken. Everything looks fuzzy through them. He left a large notebook prominently placed on his coffee table. He must have been leafing through it one last time while waiting for the ambulance to take him to the hospital, because the cover is stained with blood. Not a word is written in the notebook, only numbers in narrow columns, which make up increasingly long and complicated equations. Were these columns of numbers and incomprehensible equations the Memoirs that he wanted to write and couldn't stop rewriting? Mademoiselle Aldine didn't give the blood-stained notebook to Ma. Instead, she gives it to me because she says that all of Ma's belongings will eventually be mine.

I went back to see Ma to ask her to forgive me for not guessing right away that the commander had died. I held her in my arms, not saying a word because there isn't anything to say. Tears are streaming down her cheeks. She wanted to give me her painting, the one thing she made to which she signed her name. I didn't dare refuse because she wouldn't have understood why I don't like her painting. She would have assumed that it wasn't painted well, and would have felt even more pain. She sat back down in her armchair. Using the remote control she turned on the television again, leaving it on the nonexistent channel. I understood that she wanted me to leave.

§12
I didn't walk back along Woods Lane, which leads to the station. I don't want to return to Paris and find myself alone in my studio thinking about Ma. I wandered on the streets until I reached the quarries that separate Mells-le-Château from Mills-le-Pont. Past the quarries is a construction site filled with cranes and half-built towers. It used to be a vacant lot where I would play with Luira, my best friend as a child. The site is closed to the public. An armed guard is posted at the entrance to enforce the restriction, and he tells me I must go around another way. But once you are past the quarries, the only route to Mills-le-Pont, aside from turning around and walking for hours, is through the site. The guard sits on a folding chair in front of a cabin, which must be where he sleeps at night, and is burning a packet of letters. He watches his fire to make sure that it doesn't blaze up. I threw the commander's notebook, given to me by Mademoiselle Aldine, into the guard's fire. The guard smiled at me. He's pleased that I've made use of his fire to burn such a thick notebook. He's burning the letters that his wife wrote to him while he was a soldier at the front. She recently left him for a foreman on the site, and he wants to burn everything of hers to rid himself of the memories. He

wanted to see the painting I'm carrying under my arm. He thinks it's truly a nice painting. So without a second thought I gave it to him. I don't want Ma's self-portrait in my studio. The guard is very pleased that I gave him such a nice painting. As thanks, he allows me to enter the construction site that is closed to the public. Crossing directly through the site you reach the Poterne, the northern section of Mills-le-Pont, which lies between the canal and the railroad tracks. The guard asked me what I was going to do all alone in such an infamous neighborhood. I told him that I'm going to see the building where I lived with Ma for twenty-one years.

Crossing through the construction site, which is closed to the public, I understood why the guard didn't want to let me in. He was waiting for me to give him the customary ten francs. He thought Ma's painting was much better than ten francs. Past the half-built towers are barracks where the African construction workers live. As soon as they saw me they gestured to me to come in. They think I'm something I'm not. I passed by two African women who were already undressed. The guard is clever. When the workday is over and the foremen are gone, he closes his eyes to all the smuggling that goes on at the site, which isn't surveyed by the police because it's a guarded site. The police have plenty of work with the gangs in the Poterne, not to mention the surveillance of the canal where the mutilated bodies of two young African girls were found last year. There was a recent scandal about smuggling young Africans into parties at the home of a well-known person in Mells-le-Château who is protected by the po- lice. The guard's wife must have had her reasons for leaving. Ma will never know what I did with her painting, so she won't be hurt.

The construction site used to be a vacant lot where the vagabonds of Mells-le-Château camped. I would play there with Luira without Ma knowing. Luira would meet Luiji. For ten francs she would show him her breasts, and for twenty she would take off her underwear. Luiji lived in the nicest trailer in the vacant lot. Every night he would walk across the canal blindfolded on a tightrope. Luira reminded him of the young trapeze artist he loved in his youth, who had fallen from her trapeze right after he asked her to marry him. Blindfolded on his tightrope each night, it was as if he were searching unsuccessfully for death. I would wait for Luira on the steps of the trailer. She always wanted me to go with her so that I could have ten francs too. But I never wanted to because my breasts were so small, and I would never have dared to take off my underwear. Before going home we would buy doughnuts from Rosa, who had a little store at the entrance to the vacant lot. Apparently she wasn't selling just doughnuts, and the store served as her cover from the police. The vacant lot gave the Poterne a bad reputation and I was ashamed to tell people at school where I lived. Ma didn't want to move because the low rent made it possible for her to put money aside in case of misfortune. She had a fixation on misfortune, and because of her fixation I was haunted by the idea of misfortune.

The guard at the construction site told me that the towers were being built to rehouse the inhabitants of the Poterne. The old neighborhood is going to be torn down to make way for an artificial lake surrounded by playing fields, with pedal-boats in the summer. It's the new mayor's big project, the one that helped get him elected. He is hoping that the lake and the towers will rid Mills-le-Pont of gangs and smugglers. It's a good thing I chose today to visit the building where I grew up because soon an artificial lake with pedal-boats will be there in its place. The main street in Poterne hasn't changed, still the site of the large brickyard and, at the far end, the corner building where I lived with Ma for twenty-one years. Across the street, where the garage used to be, there is now a moving company. Ma wouldn't allow me to play at the garage with Luira because the mechanic repainted stolen cars and his wife supplied people with false papers. Luira spent all her free time in stolen cars with Mike, the mechanic's son. Every day in the back of the class she told me everything she had done the night before with Mike. Luira had already done everything with Mike. She knew all the precautions to take so that she wouldn't get pregnant or catch any diseases. She said that every time with

Mike was like going to heaven, and that she would gladly burn in hell some day for having gone to heaven so often. She educated me instead of Ma, who told me nothing.

Madame Anna, Luira's mother, was the one person Ma spoke to in our building. In addition to Ma's regular work, she made dresses for Madame Anna at night and on Sunday. I waited impatiently for the fitting days. I never tired of watching Madame Anna undress in front of the large mirror to try on her new dress. She had the body of a model. In order to pay Ma, Madame Anna received men in her room between the hours of six and seven: the foreman at the brickyard, the bookkeeper at the garage, and the landlord of the building, not to mention the town clerk, who didn't have special hours. Ma pretended not to know what was going on. She liked to make clothes for Madame Anna, who was much too elegant and distinguished to be the caretaker of a building in the Poterne. Ma, who had dreamed of being a dancer instead of a seamstress, must have felt close to Madame Anna, though they were not alike. Luira was like Madame Anna and I wanted to be like Luira.

There was no answer when I knocked on the caretaker's door, and very few names are left on the mailboxes. The building isn't kept up anymore because it's about to be torn down. Most of the tenants have already left. I climbed up to the top floor anyway to see where Ma and

I used to live. The door of the apartment is wide open and I walked in as if I were at home. I didn't recognize anything from Ma's and my old apartment. There's no furniture left and the walls are stained. I practically ran back down the stairs. Someone yelled insults at me in a language I don't understand.

I waited half an hour for the bus before remembering that the bus doesn't run on Sundays. That means I will have to walk to the station on the road that follows the canal, running along the railroad tracks. Years ago, One-Arm Roko used to park his blue Cadillac on this same road. Luira was the one who told me his name and that he was an informer protected by the police. Everyone was scared of him. With his one remaining arm, he was said to have the best aim of anyone in Mills-le-Pont. Luira liked to walk past his blue Cadillac on purpose, but I was scared.

Madame Irma, Madame Alma's sister, lived with And in a house on the road that follows the canal. Inside the house the walls trembled with every train, but outside barges passed by on the canal. I went there every Thursday because I didn't have classes. Madame Irma worked across the street at the Flood Gate Bar. Having received a disability pension from the railroad, And no longer worked. He had lost a leg in a bad accident on the tracks. He never talked about his accident, and he managed to walk on his artificial leg with almost no limp. He wouldn't resign himself to being an invalid, and he took classes in computer science.

Every Thursday I took math lessons from And so that I could be first in my class. I didn't dare move as he would press against me during the math lessons. As soon as Madame Irma returned from the bar, he would kiss her, touching her breasts. She would push away and the arguments would begin. He called her all sorts of names. She would turn the radio on loud so that I couldn't hear them. Madame Irma would tell me about her life. She had left Sise at twenty to start her singing career in Paris, and then she found herself working as a waitress at the Flood Gate Bar, where she met And, a railroad worker from Mills-le-Pont. When it was time for me to leave, she would slip ten francs in my pocket. I would hide the money from Ma and spend it at the fortune-teller's trailer with Luira. Then And would turn off the radio. I don't know what happened after that. Luira, who knew all the gossip from Madame Anna, told me that And hadn't had an accident on the tracks but that he had wanted to kill himself because Madame Irma cheated on him with clients from the Flood Gate Bar to forget that she had lost her singing voice. I never told Ma about the scenes I witnessed, fearing that she wouldn't let me return. I wanted to remain first in my class in math, and I also wanted the ten francs Madame Irma gave me so that I would have the same amount of spending money as Luira.

Madame Irma's depression began the year I left Mills-le-Pont to live with Enz in Paris. She lost her job at the Flood Gate Bar because she was too old to be a waitress there. She couldn't take being alone in the house all day with And. One day she slit her wrists and was taken to the asylum in Mills-le-Pont. She never returned, as though she preferred the asylum to the house. The last time I went to see her she gave me an envelope and asked me not to return. Her life's savings were in the envelope. She died several months later from a heart attack. Ma didn't go to her funeral. Ma never forgave Madame Irma for having made her the apprentice to a seamstress at the age of twelve when she had wanted to be a dancer. After Madame Irma died, And returned to Auvergne to live with his mother. He had failed all his computer science exams. The little house was torn down. Now a parking lot for the train station is there in its place.

As I waited on the platform for the RER to Paris, I suddenly asked myself what was going to happen to me. When Luira and I visited the fortune-teller, the fortune-teller would always say she couldn't read my future because it was written in a language she didn't know. Seeing my disappointment, the fortune-teller would say it was proof that I had a destiny. Had I been able to choose between a life and a destiny, I would have chosen a life. But, as the fortune-teller said, neither a destiny nor a life can be chosen because it's all been written before, in every language.

§13

There's a message from Kell on the answering machine. He asks me to meet him at the airport in Paris. I un- packed all my summer dresses and ironed them because they were wrinkled from having spent the winter in a trunk. I tried them on in front of the mirror to decide which one I should wear to go meet Kell. I hesitated for a long time. I found faults in each dress. In the end I chose the simplest, white linen with an orange belt.

I arrived at the airport early. I like airports even more than train stations. I ran into Curtz at the bar where I went to have a drink. He smiled as soon as he saw me as though he were waiting for me, and he insisted that I sit with him. He looks good in his white suit and pink shirt, as though he has forgotten about the tragic end to Lill's life. Curtz also likes airports, and he always arrives early in case he might run into someone. He gives me a look that makes me blush and feel ill at ease, and says with a smirk that I resemble a young girl in my white linen dress. He wants to know what I have been doing in the year since we last saw each other, and what I'm doing alone at the airport. I tell him that I haven't done anything in the last year because I haven't figured out what to do, and that today I'm meeting Kell, who is in charge of the investigation in Sise City. Laughing, Curtz asks me what possessed me to travel in the Andes last summer when I had never been to America. I know he thinks that until I visit America I won't find what I'm looking for and will never write my second novel. When I'm with Curtz I have a hard time finding the right words to say. It's hard to follow what he says because he speaks quickly, with the accent he refuses to lose because it makes him sound like an American movie star.

A voice over the loudspeaker announces the immediate departure of the flight to Sise City. Erma arrived running, accompanied by a cameraman from the cable station. Everyone turns to look. In her low-cut apple-green dress with white polka dots, she's hard to miss. She and Curtz are going to do a live broadcast from the Paradiso in Sise City. Curtz is going to talk about Witz and give a final tribute to Lill. Witz's death is a big moment for Curtz; it's as if he were alone all of a sudden – the only one left. Curtz introduced me to Erma as the author of *Sise Memories*. Erma smiled at me and caught Curtz's eye. From the way she looks at Curtz it's obvious that she wants to have an affair with him at the Paradiso. As Curtz left he said he hoped I had a good vacation and he would call me when he returned from Sise City. It's quite a coincidence that I ran into him at the airport the same day I'm there to meet Kell.

Curtz's plane took off as Kell's landed. Kell told me right away that his car was in the parking lot and that he's taking me to the beach. We took the Autoroute du Nord.

Kell drives fast because he's in a hurry to get there. He won't tell me where he's taking me, as if it were all a surprise. The autoroute is deserted. At the speed we're driving, we will be there in two hours.

Kell tells me everything he's learned in Sise City. Witz sent a letter to *Paris Night* before he died, but it can't be published because it accuses Curtz without any proof. In Witz's letter, he says that he decided to die in his jet and to disappear in the sea with his Memoirs after having lost his fortune at the casino. That he decided to die with his Memoirs shows that the life described in the Memoirs is over. Gradually he saw that his work would take on its full meaning only after the end, the one possible end. There's no mention of Lill in the letter. For the moment Kell sees no link between Witz's suicide and Lill's murder. He's on the trail of Lind, who disappeared the night of the tragedy and hasn't been heard from since. Lind was the commander's aide-de-camp when there was a military base in Sise. When the commander became the president of PAL, Lind became his personal secretary and right-hand man. Looking through files in the Interpol archives, Kell discovered that Lind and the president both served as aviators in the war in the squadron commanded by the current mayor of Rore. Witz also served in the same squadron.

Kell was not able to interrogate the president of PAL. Since his attack and his move to the nursing home, the presi-

dent no longer remembers anything except his love for Marion. Marion was found unconscious on the grave of
Father Jan and was transported to the room next to the president in the nursing home. She is fading slowly as Stev watches, sitting by her bedside. He abandoned his lighthouse, which is automated now and can run without him. Kell interrogated the members of PAL's board of directors, none of whom said anything. He learned everything he knew from Lenz, who is worried about the power the Bank of Rore has acquired in Sise City within the last year. Lenz himself is in debt to the bank for the money he borrowed to pay for the endless repairs on the Palace by the Sea. The president of PAL has been aware of the danger and saw it coming for a long time. He was secretly writing a book about the mayor of Rore, who is also the president of the bank, whom he knew well during the war. With Lind's help he accumulated all the documents and evidence against the mayor. He wanted his book to show that the mayor of Rore had been a war criminal and since that time had become one of the major smugglers. Lenz thinks that writing the book caused the president's collapse because it took so much out of him; he was never satisfied and was always missing the final piece of evidence. When the president felt that he no longer had time to finish the last chapter, he gave his manuscript to Lind to finish for him and to publish after his death. Lenz is worried about Lind's disappearance on the night of the tragedy. He doesn't understand what

it could mean. Kell still sees no explanation for Lill's murder. He is sure that Lind is his only lead and that following Lind's trail will lead to the mayor of Rore.

Kell wants to forget the case now because he's with me and we are on our way to the beach. He read *Sise Memories* on the airplane. He says that for the first time in his life he has met someone who is like him. He turned on the radio to a foreign station with inaudible voices. After a minute the voices stopped and there was only music. It's an instrumental version of *Candy*. While driving, Kell caresses me gently under my dress, then less gently until I begin to moan. We are approaching the sea. The air is cooler all of a sudden, and it smells of iodine and seaweed. Kell knows where he's going. After we got off the autoroute he turned down several small roads without hesitating and without looking at the map. At the very end of the last road is an abandoned lighthouse and a broken-down airplane hangar. The place is without a name because all the signs have disappeared. A bungalow stands in front of the hangar and has red letters that read: *Dancehall*. Kell parked the car in front of the hangar and turned off the lights. He removed a flashlight from his suitcase. In front of us, the surface of the sea is silver under the full moon. On the beach, which is so flat it seems endless, a row of seagulls sit facing the sea and seem to sleep as they keep watch.

The door to the dancehall isn't locked. It looks as though there was a raid and everyone fled. An old accordion lies on the floor. The chairs and tables surrounding the dance floor have been knocked over. The dance floor is covered in a moth-eaten red carpet. Kell asked me to undress as he did on the train the first night we met. My eyes are blinded by the flashlight he shines on me. There is no sound. The light went off suddenly and Kell pushed me over on the red carpet. He made love to me so hard, calling me Candy, that I thought I was about to die. He left the room without saying anything to me as I dressed. I joined him in the room at the top of the lighthouse. In the small room overlooking the sea, the old equipment is in place as if it still functioned. A small iron bed with a sunken mattress stands in one corner. It feels like midday with the moonlight shining into the room. Kell made me kneel on the sunken mattress with my head against the iron bars. He caressed me harder and harder until it hurt. I want what he wants. Tonight, in the small iron bed in the room at the top of the abandoned lighthouse with my mussed white linen dress pushed up, Kell made love to me as I have never been made love to before. Afterward we remained half asleep next to each other for a long time, attached to the iron bars like two prisoners without chains.

At daybreak we walked on the beach. The seagulls had already flown away. Kell kissed me gently on the lips for the first time. Before returning to the car, we went to the hangar to see the old dual-engine propeller planes that are no longer in working order. In front of the hangar, traces of the old landing strip are still visible though it's almost covered by the dunes. We got back on the autoroute heading for Paris. Kell told me that his grandfather was the last keeper of that lighthouse. Kell used to live in the dancehall with his mother, Molly. He never met his father, an aviator who left and never returned. Molly was brutally killed one night after the dancehall had closed and she was cleaning up alone, singing *Candy*. The police never found the murderer or discovered the motive behind the crime. After Molly's death, Kell's grandfather was found drowned near the lighthouse. Years later, as an adult, Kell decided to work for Interpol and to search for Molly's killer, who was also responsible for the death of his grandfather. He has to continue the search, even though he no longer knows where to look or for whom. He dropped me off in front of Notre-Dame and said goodbye. I asked him where he lived. He said he lived at the Seaport Hotel near the Porte de Choisy.

§14

I was so tired from my trip to the beach that I went to bed as soon as I got in. It was practically nighttime when I woke up. There had been a storm and the quays were wet. I pushed the window wide open. The smell of the rain-soaked trees on the quay filled my studio. There's a message on the answering machine. Bobby Wick was in Paris. He is staying at the Hôtel des Grands Hommes on the Place du Panthéon, where he lived the year he was studying at the Sorbonne. I called his room several times but there was no answer. The receptionist told me that there was a message for me. Bobby Wick had been rushed to the emergency room. He has a package for me and he wants to see me in person.

The hospital is just across the Seine from my studio. I went straight to the head nurse to find out why Bobby Wick was rushed to the hospital almost immediately upon his arrival in Paris. She asked me if I was a relative. I said no, that I was only a friend. Bobby Wick has no family and, apart from myself, he knows no one in Paris. The nurse tells me that he doesn't have long to live. His illness has spread. The only thing left to do is to give him shots of morphine to minimize the pain. The nurse realized that she had given me a shock and she offered me an orange ice. She's African and there's a singsong rhythm to her speech. Her name is Miria. She has very dark skin but her features are even and delicate like a madonna's. She doesn't look like someone who lives with death all day long. All her thoughts are of love and of her fiancé, whom she met recently and who is also African. She tells me that Bobby Wick has talked about nothing but love since he arrived.

Bobby Wick smiled at me as soon as he saw me enter the room. The blinds are drawn. His health has deteriorated so much in one year that I can barely see what is left of his gaunt face and emaciated body. He doesn't want to talk about himself; he wants to talk about me and all that I have done since the Andes. I had to tell him that I haven't done anything. He looks at me gravely and says that I must not waste time while I'm living at the heart of time because later on it will be too late and I will never be able to go back. His time has passed. All that is left for him is to say goodbye. He took me by the hand to help him remember our trip to the Andes, and the last night that we spent hand in hand watching the stars shine over the Glacier of Angels. He tells me not to die like he is, alone, without family and far from his own country. Then he opened the drawer of the bedside table and handed me a package. He doesn't want me to open it in front of him. It will be up to me to decide what to do with it. He tells me about Miria, the nurse who is taking such good care of him. Through her he's able to relive his memories of Africa for the last time. He was never able to feel comfortable in America after having lived in Africa for so long. Even though Africa killed him, he doesn't regret anything because he experienced things he never would have been able to experience had he remained in America. When he finished talking about Miria, he asked me to leave. He is very tired and no longer has the strength to talk. He doesn't want me to visit him again. He wants to spend his last days alone in his hospital room with Miria at his bedside, as though he had never left Africa.

After leaving him, I walked to the square in front of Notre-Dame and sat down on a bench so that I wouldn't have to be alone in my studio. It makes me terribly sad that Bobby Wick is about to die. Yet I only knew him one summer in the Andes and had not even written to him once since then, and had almost forgotten him. The package contains his black book. But what is written in the book isn't the transcendental poem that he wanted to compose from the words he wrote down each night in the tent. What is written is the names and addresses of the African women he knew, and in detail what he did with each one, the price he paid, and all the treatments he underwent during his illness. The writing has no style and many words are abbreviated. Why did Bobby Wick give me his black book as if it held his last words? What happened to the transcendental poem he wanted to write so that people would remember more than just Curtz's novels? It's too late for me to ask him now. The book isn't worth reading; it simply repeats the same story. The names of the African women are all that change. I threw the black book in the Seine. The strong current, caused by storms upriver, carried the book swiftly toward the sea. The water of the Seine washed away the ink in the book, erasing Bobby Wick's African adventures. Maybe his book will be swept as far as America. I looked in the direction of the hospital. All the lights are out.

The next day I went to the Bazar de l'Hôtel de Ville to buy paint and paintbrushes. I want to take advantage of my quiet summer days alone in Paris to repaint my stu- dio. I want to repaint the whole place myself so that, despite its age, it will seem new the first time Kell visits. Miria called to tell me that Bobby Wick died during the night. He didn't feel anything because she had increased his dosages of morphine each day until finally he was in a coma. He left his body to medicine to help the progress of research on African diseases. He has neither inheritance nor heirs. He doesn't want any ceremony after his death. Miria tells me that she's leaving for a vacation in Africa with her fiancé and she hopes I have a good vacation. Living in my studio with the blinds drawn to block the sun, I'm able to forget that it's summer and that everyone is leaving for vacation. I don't know why I feel that, after Bobby Wick's death, my adventure with him and this long year during which I have done nothing have been a dream from which I will awake suddenly in my newly painted studio.

There's a letter from the lawyer in Sise City under my door. Line bought Dilo and Lou's house for the same price Ma sold it to them originally. Due to the real estate crisis, the house hasn't increased in value. The sale of Dilo and Lou's house leaves me with less money than I hoped. Even if I invested my money wisely, it won't give me enough to live on and won't allow me to buy my studio.

Line will surely close the Hotel by the Sea and live in Dilo and Lou's house. She wants to take care of Stev, who has been completely lost since Marion had to move to the nursing home because she's nearing the end. Stev is writing his last poem at Marion's bedside. My newly painted studio drinks in the evening light. The image of Notre-Dame reflects off the Seine while the boats float by, their loudspeakers repeating the same speech about Notre-Dame and the bridges. Lights from the boats illuminate the facades on the quay like a movie set.

§15

Enz called me because he's passing through Paris. It was strange to hear his voice over the phone after all the time we had been apart. If he hadn't left me to move to Elms, I never would have written *Sise Memories*. His life in Elms is over now. He sold all his paintings and received a grant to go to Italy. Walking out of a movie theater on his first night back in Paris, he ran into Luira, my best friend from Mills-le-Pont. Luira lives alone now that Mike is in prison. She didn't tell Enz what Mike had done to be sentenced to twenty years. Enz thinks Luira looks even prettier than before. He invited her to go with him to Italy. She wants to forget Mike and was pleased to run into Enz outside the movie, so she accepted. Luira has always had luck in love – she takes after Madame Anna, who lived for love, unlike Ma, who lived only for me. I'm not like Ma but I have always felt divided between her character and my own because she wanted me to take after her. In the end, Madame Anna married the town clerk of Mills-le-Pont. They moved to Menton and bought a flower shop. I was ashamed to tell Enz that I haven't written anything since *Sise Memories* and that I went to see Sonia, the doctor, who arranged an extended sick leave for me because I don't want to teach at the school in Mills-le-Pont anymore. I didn't tell him about Kell because he would have said that I was crazy to be in love with an Interpol agent who is always away on dangerous missions. I'm not really crazy but it's difficult to be Candy when I've always been Mia. Enz doesn't know who Candy is so he wouldn't understand. Enz told me that I could use his grandfather's house in Elms before it's sold. He never took me to Elms and I never took him to Sise, as though neither of us had a past or a history.

I don't know what came over me when I found myself alone in my studio after Enz's phone call. I drank an entire bottle of whiskey and collapsed on the floor. When I awoke, my head was killing me and everything around me was spinning. My wedding dress, which was wrapped in silk paper and stored at the bottom of my trunk, is lying in the middle of the room. Ma spent years sewing it because she wanted it to be unique. The dress is too sumptuous to wear on regular occasions and, as I have never married, I have never worn it. But I've kept it carefully at the bottom of the trunk like a treasure. The dress is badly torn, the hooks are ripped off, and I threw up all over it. I have no memory of what happened. I thought of Madame Irma when she began to drink. She became depressed and slit her wrists after going through a detox program, then ended up at the asylum in Mills-le-Pont. All of a sudden I was scared of becoming like her. Ma always told me that I resembled Madame Irma. Ma's deepest disappointment was that I took after Madame Irma and not Madame Alma. Whenever Ma was mad that I disobeyed her, she would tell me I was going to end up like Madame Irma. I hated myself for causing Ma so much pain, when she sacrificed her life for me. I would promise myself never to disobey her again, though I loved to because she and I were complete opposites. When I think of Madame Irma, I can't see how I resembled her. I never wanted to be a singer and I always hated Mills-le-Pont. I don't want to end up like Madame Irma, someone I don't resemble.

I went for a walk along the quays to the Pont Marie. To me, Paris is the Seine and the bridges. I returned home to watch Erma's show on cable, being broadcast live from the Paradiso in Sise City. Curtz retraces Witz's life and his career. Listening to the excerpts Curtz read from *The Paradiso of Fort Amo,* I felt like crying, as if it were the story of my own life. Erma then announced Lenz's exciting new project. Madame Alma's house, which belongs to Sise City now that Will is dead, is going to be part of the Witz Foundation, under Lize's direction. When Line heard about Lenz's project, she immediately wanted to be involved, and she donated the Hotel by the Sea to Sise City so that it could be included in the foundation. Erma presents a glowing portrait of Lize: wife of the mayor of Sise City, owner of the Paradiso, and director of the Witz Foundation. It's as if Lize, in her low-cut red dress, has finally become Lill. Then Line appeared in a black satin dress. She rediscovered her ability to read aloud, as when she used to recite her poetry to the officers from the base. She reads Stev's last poem, which is not a poem about Marion but about his own death. The night Marion died at the nursing home, Stev returned to Sise City. He set out in his old boat. He went through the channel. His boat leaked, so he never made it to the maritime route to Rore. Stev chose to drown amid the reefs in the sea near the Sise lighthouse along with the old boat that used to belong to his father. He had with him the manuscripts of his poems, all of which Line had copied secretly, including the final one, which he had read to her before saying goodbye. Line says that Stev was the last great living poet. The Witz Foundation will publish a posthumous volume of Stev's poems, which neither Boston nor Moréno would publish because it wasn't a novel. Erma thanks Line for having saved such a beautiful collection of work and for having introduced this great poet – and his tragic destiny – to the television audience. Finally she reports that Curtz has just been named honorary president of the Witz Foundation and that he will write the preface to the posthumous edition of Stev's poems.

§16

For my lunch date with Kell at the Seaport Hotel I dressed in a bright red dress with shoulder straps and a white belt to match my espadrilles, as though I were on vacation at the beach. I plan to ask Kell to come with me to Elms because Enz is lending me his grandfather's house. I walked all the way to Porte de Choisy. I know the route well because Enz and I used to live in Tolbiac right near Porte de Choisy. On summer evenings we would walk along the quays to Notre-Dame, looking out at the Seine and dreaming of the sea. Today I am taking the same route in the opposite direction. Enz and I used to live at the end of an alley in a small, rented house that was covered in Virginia creeper and had a veranda and a garden. The alley belonged to Madame Lisa, once a singer at the Eldorado who had become a dealer in secondhand goods. The gossip in the alley was that the secondhand business served as Madame Lisa's cover for smuggling stolen jewels. Enz had a studio on the ground floor where he would paint. I built myself a little greenhouse in the garden where I could grow rare flowers. The same day that Enz moved to Elms after his grandfather died, I received an eviction notice from Madame Lisa. She had just sold the alley to a developer, having decided to abandon her secondhand business and try her hand at import-export. So I let my flowers die and I closed up my greenhouse. I moved to my studio overlooking Notre-Dame.

I don't recognize Tolbiac. There are towering buildings everywhere and shops selling Asian goods. A glass building stands in place of the Eldorado. Gold letters engraved on the door read *Lisa & Co. Import-Export*. Madame Lisa has come a long way from being a singer. The Seaport Hotel is at the end of an alley. There is no sign, just an inscription on the door: *Rooms for rent by the month only*. I had to ring several times before a little boy in a blue suit opened the door. As I followed him down the hall I noticed that he was limping. He leads me to a little glassed-in room that serves as a front office where Lina, his mother, is on the phone. He tells me to take a seat while I wait for her. He sits down next to me and starts talking so that I won't feel bored. His name is Li. He was never able to go to school, having spent his childhood in the hospital with a disease that affected his hips. He has a very sweet smile, as though he thought everything would come to him easily. The little glassed-in room that serves as a front office opens onto a back room with a beautiful old pool table. At the far end of the room is a door marked *Private*. Lina finished her telephone conversation. She opened the door marked *Private* with her key and asked me to follow. Li holds her hand as if she were blind and he her guide. Lina's smooth face and perfect makeup make it difficult to tell her age. Her perfume permeates the hallway. She escorts me into a small dining room reserved for guests. I never would have imagined that Kell could live in a hotel like this.

Kell arrived almost immediately. He's unshaven and his suit is wrinkled. I don't dare tell him that I'm sad not to see him more often. He doesn't even have time to show me his room. When Kell told me that he was on Lind's trail, he forgot to tell me that he knew Lind but didn't know that he was the personal secretary to the president of PAL. He knew Lind only as the man who looks after Lina. Lind met Lina after the war, when she was working at the Eldorado as an usherette, and he bought the hotel for her when the Eldorado closed. Lind saved Lina's life one night when she wanted to die. Since the tragedy in Sise City, Lina has had no news of Lind. Lina agreed to talk to Kell about Lind only after Kell mentioned the manuscript that the president of PAL had entrusted to Lind, for him to complete and publish after the president's death. Lina is scared that Lind might betray the president and negotiate a deal with the mayor of Rore for the sale of the manuscript. Since Lind found out that PAL was in bankruptcy and that the Bank of Rore was gaining power in Sise City, his one desire has been to leave Europe with Lina and Li and to begin a new life in Australia. Lind doesn't care if the manuscript is published or the mayor of Rore is exposed as long as his dream of a new life comes true.

I tell Kell that it sounds just like one of Witz's novels. He says that Witz's novels have become real since Witz's death. Lina also told Kell that Lill, when she was young and working at the Eldorado, had an affair with the mayor of Rore. Lill told Witz everything she knew, and Witz was going to expose the mayor of Rore in his Memoirs, based on Lill's testimony. Lina doesn't believe that Witz committed suicide; she thinks he was murdered. Lina believes that on the mayor of Rore's orders Trak killed Lill and Witz, as he does well, without leaving a single trace, just like in the movies. Lina used to know Trak well because she had an affair with him during the days of the Eldorado. The mayor of Rore and Trak were inseparable even then, and they were the Eldorado's two best clients. Lina told Kell that it was already too late for her to begin a new life. Li is her only reason for living. She wants to do everything she can to help Kell find Lind. It's hopeless for Lind to think his dream might come true, because the mayor of Rore is very powerful and Trak, his right-hand man, will do anything for him. Lina's reasons for helping Kell were twofold: she wants to avenge the death of Lill, her best friend from the days of the Eldorado; and she wants the mayor of Rore to be found guilty along with Trak, the man who betrayed her.

It's not the right moment to ask Kell to go with me on vacation. I told him I was going to spend the August 15 holiday on Elms. He said he would call me when I returned. Li showed me to the door, holding my hand as if to say there was nothing to worry about because he was there watching over everything like a guardian angel. Outside the sun is shining, but there is a veil over my eyes.

§17

Elms is an island lost in the middle of the sea just south of Sise. Developers have purchased most of the island and they are building marinas everywhere, as well as small harbors in all the coves. There's now an airport on Elms and a direct flight from Paris once a week, thanks to the developers. When I saw Ma's grandfather's house from the plane, a small speck by the sea, I couldn't believe I was flying over Sise. Enz always used to tell me about his grandfather's house, where he spent every summer as a child. His grandfather was the son of a fisherman who became a teacher. By going after the smugglers, who enforced their own laws, his grandfather became the first mayor of Elms to reestablish order on the island.

Enz's grandfather's house is the last house on the very tip of the northern point of the island. It's a small white house with blue shutters. Enz's grandfather always lived in the same house, even after he became mayor. I had my blank notebooks with me. Rocks surround the house, and there is a pier where a small, recently painted fishing boat rocks constantly back and forth on the rough sea. I can't tell who owns the boat because there are no other houses nearby. The house may be isolated, without a telephone or electricity, but I'm not scared. I can't tell what is in the armoires or trunks because they are all locked. Enz put everything away before leaving so that the house would be ready to sell. The sea at the northern point is too dangerous for swimming. When I'm not standing on the rocks watching the sea, I sit in the small bedroom in front of my blank notebooks. *Candy* was the first word I wrote. Not one boat is visible on the horizon, as if the sea were empty. The small boat at the pier in front of the house creaks as it rocks back and forth.

On August 15 I met Yell, the owner of the small boat. Shocked to see the shutters open, he knocked at the door. He told me that Enz became his friend and that he is lonely now that Enz has left. Yell is the lighthouse keeper on Elms. The lighthouse was built at the summit of the highest mountain in the middle of the island. On a clear day, using binoculars, one can catch a glimpse of Sise from the very top of the lighthouse. Yell goes fishing by himself on Sundays and holidays. He takes his boat way out past the northern point to where the lighthouse is no longer visible. He has never married because of a serious heart condition, from which he will soon die. He's not afraid of death. It's as if he were going out to meet his end alone in his boat. He knows he will die in his boat, like in the dream he's had every night since Enz left. He asks me who I am. I tell him that I lived with Enz before he moved to Elms, and that since then I wrote *Sise Memories*.

Because today is a holiday, Yell invited me out on his boat. He didn't take me all the way out past the northern point where he goes fishing by himself. Instead we go on a tour of the island, as if I were a tourist and he my guide. I brought along my portable video camera to film my boat ride with Yell. I filmed the marinas under construction, which resemble brand-new fishing hamlets with sailboats lined up in the coves. I filmed Yell fishing with a net. He didn't tell me how he got the scar that is clearly visible across his torso. We returned to the northern point at dusk. We remained on the deck for a long time lying next to each another in silence, watching the stars. Beams of light from the lighthouse shined on us at intervals. I don't know what came over me all of a sudden. I rolled on top of Yell and began to kiss him as I unbuttoned his shirt and his pants. He didn't resist and then he rolled on top of me. He asked me my name. I told him it was Candy. All night long he made love to me as if we were in a dream, all the time calling me Candy. At daybreak he dressed without saying a word and left. I knew he didn't want to see me again. I watched him climb the path to the lighthouse until he disappeared around a bend. He climbed at such a fast pace that it was difficult to believe that he had a serious heart condition.

I spent my last few days in Elms closed in the small bedroom, turning my blank notebooks black. Before leaving, I closed the shutters and replaced the key in the mailbox and the sign on the door that reads: *For sale. For appointment, inquire at the lighthouse.* I ran into Rotz on the plane back to Paris. He was on Elms for the whole month of August, as the guest of a collector of American art whom he met in New York while he and Curtz were covering a story for cable TV. He just finished his novel, which he faxed daily, page by page, to Boston. All that he will tell me is that it's a police novel based on real people disguised with fictitious names, and that it has a movie-like quality. In memory of Witz and in honor of Lize, the novel is entitled *The Paradiso of Sise City.* He asks me what I was doing on Elms. I tell him that I'm not a brain surgeon but the author of *Sise Memories,* published by Boston. In Enz's grandfather's house on Elms I wrote the first draft of *Candy Story,* my second novel. When we parted at the taxi stand outside the airport in Paris, Rotz told me that he has just been made editor of his own imprint at Boston, like Curtz at Moréno. Rotz already sees himself as Witz's successor.

§18

It's impossible to reach Ma because her phone is disconnected. I called Mademoiselle Aldine, who told me that the director of the Home had asked the telephone company to cancel Ma's service. In Ma's mind now, "Mia" is Madame Alma, as she was known when Ma was a little girl in Sise, and Mademoiselle Aldine is Madame Alma. To thank Mademoiselle Aldine for taking care of her, Ma gave her the wristwatch that I had given to Ma for her birthday. She has no need for it anymore because she lives in a world without time now that the commander is dead. When the sun is out, Mademoiselle Aldine takes Ma for walks along Woods Lane next to the racetrack. Ma holds on to Mademoiselle Aldine with one arm as she leans on her cane with the other. Her balance is off and her legs continue to weaken. On their walks Ma tells Mademoiselle Aldine her most recent dream – always the same one. She climbs on board a white sailboat where all the other passengers are newlyweds.

Curtz called to invite me to his house on Quai d'Orléans for a drink. I accepted because we're neighbors, and because I'm curious to find out what his next proposition will be. He lives on the top floor of the corner building and has a large terrace with many flowers overlooking Notre-Dame. He greeted me in a small sitting room filled with old engravings. In an alcove surrounded by mirrors at the far end of the sitting room is a red velvet sofa, in front of which is a video screen. Curtz asked me into the sitting room for a private viewing, not to discuss his engravings. Curtz didn't go with Erma to Sise City solely for the opportunity to evoke Witz's and Lill's memories on cable. He was also invited by Lize. Curtz immediately felt close to Lize, who was like a substitute for Lill. Lize invited Curtz to Sise City to discuss her videotape collection, as though she knew that he was a collector and would be interested. Video is the secret passion of both Lenz and Lize. For the parties Lize organizes at the Para- diso, she installed a small closet, strategically placed and covered by a one-way mirror, from which she can film everything without being seen. As organizer, Lize never attends the parties; she disappears into her closet with her camera as soon as things are underway. Lize's videotapes allow Lenz to watch all the parties at the Paradiso – which he, as mayor of Sise City, can't risk attending – on a big screen in his large, cork-paneled office in the Town Hall. These private viewings in the safety and solitude of his large office have become his second passion, which he's able to satisfy with help from Lize. He wants to forget the Palace by the Sea and the constant financial drain of end- less repairs. Lize suggested selling her videotapes to pay off the loan from the Bank of Rore. Lize was right about Curtz. He accepted the merchandise immediately, with- out even discussing the price. He wants to create a video library at Moréno, starting with a series called *The Para- diso of Sise City,* to be released simultaneously with Rotz's first novel of the same name, published by Boston.

When Curtz turned on one of Lize's videotapes, I sud- denly understood his intentions. Curtz doesn't share Lenz's passion for solitary viewings. He wants us to act out what is playing on the screen, so that I can use the experience to write a novel for his new imprint, from which he will produce a series of videotapes. He didn't anticipate my reaction because he knew the scene in *Sise Memories* in which the heroine, a young singer from Sise hoping to obtain a contract at the Eldorado in New York, and an American producer do in fact act out what's playing on a screen in an alcove of the producer's home. Curtz took me for the heroine of *Sise Memories*. When I said that it was getting late and that I should be going, he became flushed with anger. He tells me that I have just blown my second chance to be published in his imprint, and that I will never write my second novel because I understand nothing about America or video. I had just enough time to fix my hair on my way down the stairs – I didn't even think to call the elevator.

Outside, I breathed deeply the air off the Seine. Seagulls are flying overhead just like at the beach. Now that Witz is dead and Rotz wants to take his place at Boston, Rotz has become Curtz's competition. But Curtz isn't worried. He has the advantage of dual citizenship, extensive experience, and vast know-how. Curtz is in the process of conquering Sise City with the help of Lize, whose affections Curtz won easily as the only person she could want after Witz, even if she feels some attraction toward Rotz. Curtz recently purchased the small house on the Island of the Birds to spend his weekends far from the Quai d'Orléans. He also bought a motorboat to take him home after late nights at the casino at the Palace by the Sea. Unlike Witz, who lost everything at the casino in Sise City, Curtz won each night he played. For the first time in his life Curtz feels all-powerful, and he believes blindly in his star shining in the sky above the Island of the Birds.

Before our evening turned sour, Curtz told me about Marion's death. She died in the nursing home the same night as the president of PAL. They were both buried in the new cemetery in Sise City beside the railroad tracks, according to the president's will. Toward the end, the president completely forgot about his long affair with Lou and remembered only Marion. Lenz gave a long speech to honor the memory of the president of PAL, the last commander of the base in Sise and an aviator during the war. Lenz recalled the Hotel by the Sea during the days when Marion sang *Candy*. In tracing the history of Sise City, Lenz didn't mention the base or PAL, which no longer exist. To Lenz's mind, the history of Sise City includes the draining of the marsh, the discovery of oil, the establishment of the amusement park and the casino that is open day and night, and now the Witz Foundation. Lenz didn't mention the Palace by the Sea, now under threat of collapse despite recent construction, or the Bank of Rore, which increased its power in Sise City with the recent takeover of PAL. At the end of Lenz's speech he welcomed Curtz, a new citizen of Sise City whom he wants as an adviser. The era of the president of PAL is over. Crossing the Pont Saint-Louis, I realized that it had taken more than a year since our first encounter at Seventies for me to know Curtz.

There's a message from Kell on the answering machine. He asks me to meet him on Sunday at the Excelsior in Rore.

§19

Rore is a port that is developing rapidly since oil was discovered off its coast. Just inland is Rore City with its futuristic towers, among them the Bank of Rore building, which dominates the skyline like a giant spire. The old city is built on an island and is accessible from Rore City through a subterranean tunnel. At the center of the island stands the Excelsior, the oldest hotel on the coast. The porter gave me a message from Kell. There are flowers in every vase in the room, which is on the top floor with a view overlooking the port. The valet carries my bag and tells me that Kell ordered the flowers. Kell's message says to meet him in the Excelsior bar at eleven o'clock. He also tells me to make the most of my Sunday in Rore by visiting the old city. He drew a map with arrows marking a path because it's easy to get lost in the old city of Rore.

Thinking about the evening to come, I spent the day following Kell's path through the old city of Rore. I visited Lacemakers Quay with its old wooden houses. The houses, shutters closed, have *For Sale* signs on their doors. I entered number 1, which had an "x" over it on Kell's map. It's the only house on the quay that's open to the public. It has been transformed into the Lace Museum.

The guard who sells me my ticket is very old and is dressed in a new lighthouse keeper's uniform. There is no guided tour. The lacemakers' trousseaux are on display. They are handed down, each generation adding a piece, and carefully preserved, never being used. Diamond Merchants Street is the long stretch at the end of Lacemakers Quay. The shops are closed because it's Sunday, and their iron gates are lowered. It's impossible even to look in the windows. The streets are as empty as a ghost town. I remembered the diamond that Ma gave me for my birthday and that I still haven't put to any use. Upon my return to Paris I will go to the jeweler on the Place Vendôme as Ma had asked, to have *Ma for Mia* engraved inside the ring as she wished.

Diamond Merchants Street leads to the watchtower facing the sea. It's all that's left of the fort of Rore, which was almost completely destroyed after the war. The tower is now the Rore Museum of Art. Kell marked an "x" on the tower, indicating that I should visit it. The museum is closed on Sunday but the room at the top of the tower is open. That room offers the best view of the port of Rore, as well as an exhibition of the museum's recent acquisitions. The guard is dressed in the same new lighthouse keeper's uniform worn by the guard at the Lace Museum. It's all part of a project by the mayor of Rore to commemorate the hundredth anniversary of the Rore lighthouse, the oldest and largest lighthouse on the maritime route.

In the past, the lighthouse signified to sailors that they had arrived safe and sound, and that their voyage through the dangerous reefs was over. The lighthouse was recently renovated and fully computerized. Ma's painting hangs on the wall facing the lighthouse in the exhibition room at the top of the tower. It's the self-portrait that I gave to the guard at the construction site because I didn't want it in my studio. The guard is more of a crook than I thought to have sold Ma's painting as though it were the work of a talented unknown painter. I sat on the little bench for a long time staring at Ma's self-portrait as though I were trying to figure out everything I didn't understand about her.

Back at the Excelsior I took a bath and put on my Givenchy dress. I still haven't worn it and I want to wear it tonight for Kell. After eleven o'clock, guests at the Excelsior dress formally. I waited until eleven o'clock, watching the reflection of the port in the large mirrors inside the room. The sky became pink and then slowly gray as the lights of the port turn on. Oil tankers steer away from Rore, heading in the direction of the maritime route, lit by beams from the lighthouse. Oil-drilling rigs are visible off the coast of Rore, floating like houses in the middle of the sea, their platforms illuminated as if for a celebration.

The telephone rang. It's eleven o'clock. This is the first time I've seen Kell in a tuxedo. The Excelsior bar resembles the bar of an ocean liner. Kell ordered champagne and asked the piano player to play *Candy*. He handed me a small package. It's a present for me, an antique silver ring inlaid with tiny diamonds, which he bought from an old diamond merchant in Rore. He asked that *Kell for Candy* be engraved inside the ring. He put it on the ring finger of my left hand. I'll wear the diamond Ma gave me on my right hand.

It wasn't until late that night, after we danced to all the piano player's songs and drank all our champagne, that we went upstairs to our room and Kell told me about his Sunday in Rore. Lind had finally called Lina, asking her to close the Seaport Hotel and to bring Li and join him in Rore, where he was hiding at 1 Diamond Merchants Street. The mayor of Rore just offered to buy the president of PAL's manuscript at the price Lind was asking. Lind wanted to use the down payment on the manuscript to take Lina and Li with him on the next ocean liner to Australia. After receiving Lind's call, Lina decided not to join Lind but to give Kell the address where Lind was hiding. Lind is no longer the man she knew, having betrayed the president of PAL, whose right-hand man he'd been and to whom he owed everything. Lina also wants to avenge the death of Lill, her best friend from the days of the Eldorado. She plans to sell the Seaport Hotel and to move with Li to Narbonne to live with her brother, who recently purchased a service station. When Kell arrived at

1 Diamond Merchants Street, he immediately noticed that the door to the back room wasn't closed as it should have been. Lind had just been shot through the head. His empty attaché case was still in his hand. The mayor of Rore had set a trap for Lind. He led Lind to believe that he would accept Lind's offer, only to surprise him at the moment Lind thought he'd won. The mayor sent Trak to kill Lind and destroy the manuscript. The mayor of Rore beat the president of PAL the same way he beat Witz and Lill, who had betrayed him for Witz. The Bank of Rore will continue to take over Sise City. Kell's investigation will continue until he finds Trak. Trak has always been a dark shadow beside the mayor of Rore.

It still feels like a summer night, very warm with only a light breeze. In the large mirror at the foot of the bed we can see the reflection of the roadstead, illuminated with stars that shine high in the sky and deep in the sea. I told Kell all about Bobby Wick. I have no regrets about what didn't happen on the Glacier of Angels, because it was supposed to happen with Kell at the Excelsior in Rore. The next day we flew together for the first time back to Paris. Kell asked the taxi driver to let me off in front of Notre-Dame. I invited him to see my studio. He said he didn't have time. He wants to get to the Seaport Hotel before Lina and Li have left for Narbonne, to tell Lina what had happened to Lind and to ask her about Trak.

Mademoiselle Aldine is sitting in an armchair next to Ma. It feels like nighttime in the room because the shutters are closed. A candle burns on the bedside table. Ma's heart stopped beating moments after she felt faint. Ma's eyes are closed. In her white nightgown, she looks as though she's asleep. On the bedside table next to the candle are the earrings that the commander gave Ma for her birthday. She began to feel faint right after she took off her earrings, as she did each night before going to bed. I can't believe Ma is dead. I feel as if I'm dreaming and Ma will wake up when I do. Suddenly Mademoiselle Aldine slumped forward in her chair. She fell asleep with her hand in Ma's.

I wanted to take care of everything by myself. I laid out Ma's body and did her hair. I put a headband in her hair, the one with gold threads that Mademoiselle Aldine had given to her as a birthday present. I dressed Ma in her Chanel suit and matching embroidered blouse, exactly the same clothes she had worn on her birthday. I put the earrings back on her ears, the only ones she had ever worn. Mademoiselle Aldine wanted Ma to wear the wristwatch from the jeweler on the Place Vendôme because it was my last birthday present to Ma. Mademoiselle Aldine first removed the battery. I spent the whole night by Ma's bedside watching her, as she had watched me when I was a little girl afraid of dying in my sleep. The past no longer exists now that Ma is dead.

This September 21 is a day I will never forget. The sky is threatening rain for the first time in weeks, and the air is almost cold from the wind that has been blowing throughout the night. Ma was buried in the cemetery in Mills-le-Pont. Mademoiselle Aldine and I were the only ones at the funeral, which was held at the entrance to the cemetery without any religious ceremony. Mills-le-Pont and Mells-le-Château have adjoining cemeteries. The entrance in Mills-le-Pont is next to a factory with large chimneys that billow smoke into the sky. But from the far end of the cemetery the factory is no longer visible; only the chestnut trees and the aspens of the woods are in view. Ma was buried at the far end of the cemetery in the last row facing Mells-le-Château. Mademoiselle Aldine cried. I give her my arm to lean on because she can barely stand. When the casket was lowered into the grave, Mademoiselle Aldine lay down a lily and I a rose. Then we closed our eyes until the earth covered the casket and the lilies and roses covered the earth. I asked the marble worker to engrave in gold letters on her tombstone:

Mia for Ma
Forever

After the funeral I helped Mademoiselle Aldine pack, and I accompanied her to the Gare de l'Est. Having recently turned sixty, Mademoiselle Aldine has decided to leave the Home and move to the Ardennes to live with her sister. I gave all Ma's dresses to Mademoiselle Aldine. She's the same size as Ma and has a similar figure. Mademoiselle Aldine has never had the chance to wear such beautiful dresses. Perhaps she will never wear them and will keep them in her armoire as remembrances of Ma. I packed up the rest of Ma's things to donate to the needy. All I kept was the photo album that Ma looked through each night before going to sleep. It was the book she kept by her bedside, and to her it represented all books. The album contains photos of Ma and Madame Alma in Sise, and Ma and me in Mills-le-Pont. As Mademoiselle Aldine boarded the train, we embraced without a word. I stood on the platform for a long time after the train departed as though I were waiting for someone. Only then did I cry.

§21

I took a taxi straight to the Seaport Hotel. The sign that read *Rooms for rent by the month only* was gone. In its place is a *For sale* sign. The door and shutters were closed. I rang the doorbell but no one answered. Kell left without telling me where he was going. It's pouring rain. I walked home along the quays. The rain does me good even though it's cold and I'm wet. There is a crowd of people on Pont de l'Archevêché, blocking access to the quay. A woman has jumped off the bridge into the Seine. The firemen are giving her mouth-to-mouth resuscitation. Her dog is crying next to her. I didn't slow down because I can't stand the sight of drownings. Because the firemen arrived very quickly and a young man jumped into the Seine after her, the woman has a chance of surviving.

I stopped to buy *Paris Night.* The headline in large print reads: *SUICIDE AT RORE.* The reporter who wrote the article thinks that Lind is the killer who massacred Lill in Sise City. Before committing suicide, Lind sent a letter to *Paris Night* in which he accused himself of Lina's murder. She was found dead yesterday in the bathroom of the Seaport Hotel – killed by the same method as Lill. The article stated that Lind had been mentally unstable since his days at the military base in Sise and that his mental state only deteriorated after PAL went bankrupt. According to the article, Lind's suicide is the end to the investigation in Sise City. Directly under the article on Lind is one on Curtz. Erma is angry at Curtz because, after their work on the live broadcast from Sise City, Curtz preferred Lize to her. Erma wants revenge and she has threatened to expose secrets about Curtz, which he allegedly revealed to her one night at the Paradiso. Boston has agreed to publish Erma's secrets as part of Rotz's imprint. Rotz hates Curtz because Lize chose Curtz over him, and he has decided to join forces with Erma. In Paris, Erma is the one with power, not Lize. When questioned, Curtz responded that Erma's statements were pure fiction.

I returned to my studio and lay down in all my clothes. There's no message from Kell on the answering machine. I can't help thinking of Li and what will happen to him now that Lina has been killed just like Lill, whose murder Lina wanted to avenge. I turned on the television to see

the latest developments on the news. I immediately recognized the place Kell took me the night I met him at the
airport. The headlights of an ambulance shine through
the fog and I recognize the abandoned dancehall and the
airplane hangar, in front of which are the traces of the old
landing strip. Kell never told me what that beach with no
signs was called, as though it didn't have a name. Suddenly, the lighthouse appeared on the screen. Two men
are carrying a stretcher from the lighthouse, followed by
two policemen. The man on the stretcher is covered in a
gray blanket. It's Kell. He was shot in the head like Lind.
How could Kell have known that Trak was waiting for
him at the top of the lighthouse? Kell was powerless
against Trak.

I turned off the news because I didn't want to hear any
commentary by the reporter. My studio was completely
dark. I feel as if I were about to lose consciousness and as
if everything were over. The only thing for me to do now
that Ma is dead and Kell has been killed is to write the
second draft of *Candy Story*, so that everyone will know
the real mayor of Rore. After that, I don't know.

About the Author

Born in 1948 to a seamstress and a functionary of the Parisian public transport system, Marie Redonnet was trained as a teacher but soon left her job in a public school in the suburbs of Paris in order to devote herself to writing. Since 1985, the year of the appearance of her first literary work – *Le Mort & Cie,* a set of Haiku-like verses evoking, in a considerably transfigured form, her father's death – she has published short stories (*Doublures*), novels and novellas (*Splendid Hôtel, Forever Valley, Rose Mélie Rose* [already published in translation by the University of Nebraska Press], *Silsie, Candy Story, Nevermore*), and dramatic works (*Tir et Lir, Mobie-Diq, Seaside*).

Redonnet's is one of the most distinctive voices in contemporary French literature. She is often referred to in connection with other young French writers who began to be published in the 1970s and 1980s, including Jean Echenoz, Jean-Philippe Toussaint, and Annie Ernaux. Her stark, declarative prose evokes some vast and terrifyingly complicated machinery against which her characters must struggle. Small wonder that Redonnet sees her writing as a series of parables: the subject of her work is nothing less than the world as a whole and all its invisible but inescapable workings.

JORDAN STUMP

In the European Women Writers Series